TEARS OF SORROW

Other Books By This Author

TEARS OF SORROW

D. A. Swanson

To Mom,

Enjoy the read.

D A Swanson
9/8/18

RPR

Rainy River Press
6106 Birch Road
Prior Lake MN 55372

Tears Of Sorrow

Copyright © 2018 D.A. Swanson

Cover Image Edward S. Curtis, courtesy of the Library of Congress

Print ISBN: 978-0-9863267-4-5
E-book ISBN: 978-0-9863267-5-2

This is a work of fiction. Substantial Research lends credibility to historic events while placing fictional characters as participants in those events.

First Edition: June 2018

Printed in the Unites States of America

Published by
Rainy River Press
6106 Birch Road
Prior Lake, MN 55372

Acknowledgements

My sincere thanks go out to my many friends who have helped me along the path to completing this story, and to my wife, Diane, who granted me the alone time to write it.

Once again, I am grateful for the wisdom and efforts of my editor, Jenifer Quinlan, Historical Editorial– jennyq@historicaleditorial.com Her knowledge and courage in pointing out areas needing further development, kept me on the right path. Thank you JennyQ.

The maps of the Sioux treaty lands as defined in the Fort Laramie Treaties of 1851 and 1868 were provided Courtesy of the North Dakota Studies Program, State Historical Society of North Dakota.

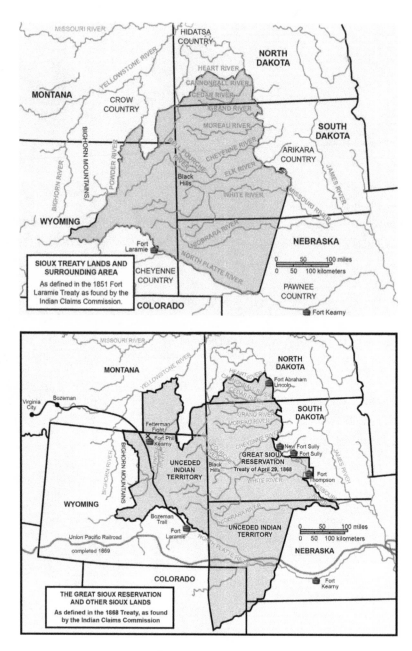

1851—1868 Fort Laramie Treaty Lines

The Great Sioux Nation

Oyate - The People

Oceti Sakowan
Seven Fire Places of the Sioux Nation

Dakota/Santee/Eastern Dakota (4-subgroups)
- **1)** Mdewakanton
- **2)** Wahpeton
- **3)** Wahpekute
- **4)** Sisseton

Nakota/Yankton/Central Dakota (2-subgroups)
- **5)** Yankton
- **6)** Yanktonai

Lakota/Teton/Western Dakota
- **7)** Teton (7-subgroups)
    - Oglala
    - Sicangu/Brule
    - Hunkpapa
    - Miniconjou
    - Sihasapa/Blackfoot
    - Itazipacola/Sans Arc
    - Oohenonpa/Two Kettle

Table of Contents

Prologue

December 29, 1890

Beneath an overcast December sky, the lone Dakota watched as the cannons fired into the makeshift camp in the depression to the south. He had never before experienced what he felt at this moment: hollow, numb, sadness so powerful he could hardly sit his horse. Old women, joints stiffened with age, were unable to run for their lives, while younger women gathered their children to flee but had no place to go. Fighting-age men were being targeted, and bullets ripped through bodies, spitting up dirt as they hit the frozen ground beyond.

He stared, unbelieving, at what was taking place below as the bile began to rise. Brave men, weaponless men under a flag of surrender, were being slaughtered indiscriminately. Women and children were raked with shrapnel as the Hotchkiss guns opened fire. Small bodies were trampled under hooves lined with steel, and blood soon covered the ground.

Then there was silence, absolute silence, as though his ears were stuffed with clay, as if his mind refused to accept the cacophony that punctuated the horrible scene. As though in a dream, he saw the smoke from the big guns and from the firearms carried by the troopers, but there was no sound. The open mouths of innocent women screaming for their children were silent. He leaned over and retched. Sweat froze on his forehead. His mind was shutting out the reality of the moment as though he were alone. Then, from what seemed to be a great distance, he heard the sounds of battle returning.

Again, he looked toward the camp until he could take no more. He reined his horse, nudged her flanks with his heels, and began to move to the north, the terrible sounds of slaughter again ringing in his ears, totally unable to process what was happening. For the first forty yards or so, he walked the roan mare. Within a hundred yards, she was at a dead run as tears cut paths along the icy skin on his temples. He had seen death a hundred ways, had taken many lives himself, but this was something his mind could not grasp. This was not a battle; there was no honor in killing the innocent. Every fiber of his being screamed for release from the agonizing scene. With his mind reeling from the sheer barbarism evidenced by this needless slaughter, he wondered at the events that had led him to this moment, to the death of the free Sioux Nation.

CHAPTER ONE

The Beginning

Dakota Territory
December 28, 1862

Four riders crossed the open prairie toward a clump of trees in the distance. Leading them was a Mdewakanton Dakota woman named Star Woman. Spread behind her, three abreast, were her husband, Anton McAlister, her son, Four Wings, and Anton's best friend, a Dakota brave namd Tatemina. Tatemina had received a last-minute pardon from President Abraham Lincoln that saved him from being the thirty-ninth man to fall into eternity in the largest mass execution in the nation's history. The executions had been the result of the short US-Dakota war of 1862, and the four were riding west to start over and escape the white backlash that followed the war.

The bitterly cold wind sweeping the prairie and hitting them head-on since the start of their journey was now beginning to subside. They had been riding since mid-morning and were anxious to find a place to camp for the night. The terrain over which they had ridden was primarily flat land with the occasional outcropping of exposed rock and little else by which to judge their progress. Some time earlier they had seen a grove of trees in the distance, and it offered the promise of shelter for the first night of their journey. They urged their horses into a canter, eager for the day to come to a close.

To the right of where they rode was a nondescript hillock, barely worth noticing as they concentrated on the grove where they intended to make camp for the night.

Suddenly, frozen ground erupted, spraying Anton's horse's belly with shards of icy soil, followed by the crack of a rifle. Another, then another shot followed in quick succession, kicking up dirt but missing the intended targets. The four riders slammed their moccasin heels against the horses' flanks, urging more speed, and dashed toward the trees, now a short distance ahead.

* * *

The hill the riders had ignored was topped with an irregular ring of stunted cedars, behind which was a natural bowl nearly sixty yards across. It was as though some giant had intentionally scooped out the dirt and stone to make the depression in the hilltop. The land was sprinkled with boulders rising stoically from the snowy patched surface of the naked earth. On the southwest rim of this bowl, a small figure lay watching the four riders as they rode to the west. His hand gently caressed the lock mechanism on the rifle he held as he watched the four Indians—representing eight hundred dollars—riding in his direction.

He was a bounty hunter named Arnold Quarterman, short in stature yet one of the most deadly men ever to ply that trade. Completely lacking a moral compass, he earned his living hunting men, initially pursuing those with a price on their heads. The Dakota Sioux uprising in Minnesota had resulted in bounties being offered on Dakota scalps, and Arnold saw a way to greatly improve his earnings.

Lying on the hill, it became clear that the four would pass at the outer limit of his rifle's accuracy. His years as a bounty hunter had endowed him with unparalleled skill at shot placement. The rifle he held had not been tested at this range; however, confident in his abilities, he aligned the sights and squeezed off the first round.

* * *

Anton yelled to the others, "Go for the trees! I'll drop off and work my way back to them." As they entered a dip in the ground, Anton, Kentucky rifle in hand, vaulted from the roan, somersaulted upon landing, and, crouching as low as he could, ran to the right, following the depression which now shielded him. The other three rode on, his horse continuing to run with them.

As near as he could figure, the firing had come from the hill just north of where they rode. He looked for at least two men, judging from the close repetition of the shots.

Anton heard the next bullet hit as frozen ground spit into the air, followed by a rifle report. Instinctively, Anton dove to the ground as another bullet slammed dirt into the air a mere eight inches to his right. Particularly unnerving was the fact that the earth had erupted before he heard the rifle report. Finally, he realized, *They're figuring out the distance!*

As he gathered himself to sprint for the cover afforded by the half dozen cedars growing to his right, a voice came from behind, "Go! Now!"

Tatemina and Four Wings had circled back, and they fired their rifles in the direction the shots had come from while Anton jumped to his feet and dashed to cover. Rather than stopping at the cedars, he continued at a dead run until he reached the exposed shale of the hill to the north from where the firing had come.

Two more shots came from the tree line that went unanswered from the hill.

Anton crept to the far side and peeked around the edge of the outcropping. There was an unnerving silence that seemed completely out of place, and he felt a shiver at the back of his neck. Where he expected to find three shooters, there was no one. The hillside was empty.

Stepping back into concealment, he rested the back of his head on the edge of the outcropping. *What is going on? Where did they go?* As the moments passed, he heard hoofbeats in the distance. Pivoting, he darted to the left where he could see the prairie they had just ridden over. There, a mere hundred yards distant, a single rider was racing away.

Bringing his rifle to his shoulder, he drew a bead on the escaping rider. As he began to apply pressure to the trigger, he started to doubt the need to kill the fleeing person. *Why, that ain't nothing but a kid.*

He lowered the rifle and scanned the area, fully expecting to see at least two more of the men who had tried to kill them. There was no one in sight. Stepping into the open, he beckoned the others to join him.

"I can't figure it. Ain't nobody run but a little kid. I don't know where the others are that were shooting at us; they didn't just disappear into thin air," he said to Tatemina, the first to reach the small hill.

"Let's take a look around and find out how they got away without us seeing 'em."

Joined by Four Wings, the three men examined the entire area and came to an unsettling conclusion.

"These tracks don't lie. There was only one person here. Them shots he fired musta come from different guns." Four Wings seated himself on an elevated slab of stone.

Tatemina answered, "I seen lots of strange things, but I ain't never seen a man carry more'n one rifle. It just don't figure. How'd he do it?"

Anton, still looking for answers, was going over the area a second time when his eyes caught something unnatural lying next to a clump of brown grass.

"I'll be damned; I think I know what happened here. Take a look at what I found over— whoa, here's a couple more."

Four Wings and Tatemina hurried to his side.

"Looks to me like whoever was doing the shooting had more than a muzzleloader." Anton held three brass bullet casings for them to see. "I'd say this guy's got one of them new breechloaders." He looked closely, examining the brass. "Now I regret not taking that shot when I saw him hightailing it outta here. I figured he was a kid, maybe even a woman. Don't matter much; I shoulda taken the shot."

"Well, what do we have here?" Four Wings said. Hidden behind a small scrubby bush was a canvas bag containing many unfired bullets of the same caliber as the casings found on the ground. "It sure looks like he was well stocked with ammunition."

Inspecting the area closer, Anton saw where the shooter had mounted a horse, and, following the tracks to the point that opened up onto the plain, he saw what looked like a metal rod bridging two substantial boulders, each with highly irregular surfaces. Stepping closer, he realized it was the barrel of a rifle. A low whistle escaped his lips.

Plucking the rifle from where it had landed, he held it aloft for the other two to see. "That had to have been one scared fella. Look what he left behind."

* * *

Arnold had been in more difficult straits, but there was something about the way the man had been able to charge straight to where he was hiding that completely unnerved him. Admittedly, the shot was a stretch—likely the longest he had ever taken—but he had never failed to hit the target before. For the first time in his life, he had looked death in the eye—not in a conventional manner, but from a distance. It was as though death had been charging toward him, every step bringing him closer to the cold, cold ground, never to be warm again. And Arnold had missed him three times.

With escape the only thing on his mind, he had dashed to the incline where he had tied his mount and stepped into the saddle. Without a thought, he'd yanked the reins and spun the horse, kicking her while slapping her on the flank with his rifle barrel, and charged out of the natural cut exiting the rock promontory from which he had fired at the four riders. He'd prayed that the rise would shield him from the charging Indian until he was out of range. He was more afraid than he had ever been.

He'd felt it slip from his grasp, but, fully consumed by the need to escape and too afraid to stop and retrieve it, the rifle he coveted had clattered among the boulders on the side of the trail.

He rode with no thoughts whatsoever beyond escape. Fear had total control of his actions. His mind blurred as he rode east. There was nothing that registered except he knew he must ride, which he did, the whole time urging speed from his mount. Eventually, he slowed his horse to a walk and his mind turned inward.

What the hell happened back there? I ain't never missed before. All them's that I kilt with never a miss, and now, here I am ridin' for my life. This ain't right. To top it off, I lost that rifle what I took from that guy awhile back. Damn it, this ain't good.

With nightfall, the wind died and the temperature fell. The sky was alive with stars, the Milky Way in full glory as it spanned the heavens. Arnold stopped long enough to pull a wool trapper's coat from his saddlebag. With the absence of wind, the temperature was bearable as long as he kept the coat tightly buttoned. His plan was to reach the settlement of Clark, where he would settle in until the weather warmed enough to comfortably resume his journey to find Henry Sibley, collect for the three scalps in his saddlebag, and buy a new rifle.

* * *

The campfire radiated heat, reflecting off the face of the large boulder, warming the four seated with their backs to the rock. Star Woman had picked the site, which lay in a slight depression surrounded by trees. The heat was welcome after riding into the wind for a solid day. It allowed them to thaw their bodies and loosen joints stiffened during the long exposure.

The four of them had dissected the earlier episode and come to the conclusion that the shooter must have been a man, albeit the smallest Anton had ever seen. His height and build were that of a twelve-year-old.

"Where do you think that little man picked up the rifle?" Tatemina asked between bites of thawed jerky.

"No way of knowing. It's a beauty, for sure. I still can't believe he got them shots off like he did. Don't matter much anyhow, him running like a rabbit. I don't figure we'll be seeing him again. Especially not without his special gun."

The sun was well below the horizon, and the air had a bite to it. Anton pulled his buffalo robe a little tighter around his shoulders. "How many days' ride you figure till we reach the hills?" He directed the question to Tatemina.

"I figure if we ride hard, it'll take us near seven days to reach the Black Hills. But with this weather, it won't be good to get the horses lathered up, so I'd guess eight to nine days of good solid travel."

"I hope it isn't much more than that," Star Woman interjected. "We've got grain for the horses for about a week. It goes beyond that, and we'll have to find something along the way. I think we will all be tired of dried meat by the time we get there. I'm hoping we can find some fresh game on the trail."

Anton rose to stoke the fire while Star Woman and Four Wings cleared a small area for them to move the fire closer to the boulder wall. Tatemina was already heading for the tree line in search of firewood sufficient to last through the night. By the time he returned, the others had pushed the hot coals to within feet of the rock wall.

"I think we stack this fire good and high, let it burn hot, and heat up this boulder."

They had each used the technique in the past to survive below-freezing nights in previous winters. As Tatemina piled dry logs on the growing fire, they helped stoke it.

With flames shooting five feet into the clear, cold air, they were forced to move away from the intense heat now being absorbed by the boulder a reach away. They watched as the fire burned until it reached a suitable size to allow them to push the coals away from the wall and spread their bedrolls on the heated ground near the boulder. The four of them bedded down under the warmth of reflected heat and were asleep within minutes.

* * *

Arnold Quarterman rode through the night. As he rode, his mind focused on the missed shots, reliving the events time and time again. Eventually, the nightmare lapsed, and he began to recount his life and how he had come to be in this position.

The second born, he knew he was a disappointment to his father. Unlike his older brother, a near mirror image of the old man, big boned and sturdy, Arnold had gotten his mother's genes; small in stature, bordering on dainty. Deemed useless for fieldwork, he was the butt of jokes by the other two and teased relentlessly. When he turned seven, the abuse became physical. At fifteen, he left the house one morning and never returned.

In order to survive in a world of bullies, he needed to find a way to earn a living. He knew that manual labor was not his thing, but over time he realized that with a deck of cards he could compete with anyone. He was fortunate in that he also received his mother's sharp mind, which he put to good use to explore and fabricate devices to level the playing field. Arnold became a professional card cheat.

His diminutive persona worked in his favor. Those being cheated viewed him as a child—a very smart child, but a child nonetheless. There was no suspicion that he was a cheat. Before long, he had several devices aimed at turning the odds in his favor as he moved from town to town visiting saloons and gambling halls.

He played with shaved decks, marked decks, and loaded dice; he learned to read people, sometimes partnering up with another thief, sharing the table, and splitting the profits. He became an expert at palming cards—replacing a loser with one that would make him a winner. He even developed a mechanism to wear under a loose-fitting sleeve that would deliver a card to his hand when he activated a trigger.

He worked the Green Bay settlements until the law appeared, and then he moved west, settling in the town of St. Paul in the newly formed state of Minnesota. During a game in Svenska Dalen, also known as Swede Hollow, a community on the outskirts of St. Paul, he killed a man who caught him palming a king of hearts to fill a flush. Rather than locking him up, the local law paid him a bounty on the man he killed for a murder he had committed in the state of Illinois.

For Arnold, a light turned on. He had stumbled upon a far more lucrative vocation. Over the next four years, Arnold Quarterman became the most feared bounty hunter west of the Mississippi. Trading in his close-quarter firearms, he became an expert with the rifled-barrel musket. His intellect enabled him to track and kill many men without risk of personal harm. He simply picked the time, lined them up in his sights, and shot them dead from a distance.

One of his victims, a thief and murderer, had escaped from an Ohio jail and he was carrying the latest breechloading rifle and a thousand rounds of ammunition he had stolen from an army dispatch scout. The Henry .44-caliber lever-action repeating rifle was capable of firing sixteen bullets without reloading, and it became Arnold's prized possession.

His fame as a bounty hunter spread almost overnight as he worked the frontier, tracking and killing wanted men. Then came the day in August 1862 that a man named Henry Sibley sent word that he wanted to meet.

When he'd first met Colonel Sibley, he was seated behind a substantial desk. He laid the papers he was reading aside and looked at Arnold. "Mr. Quarterman, your name was given to me by Governor Ramsey. It seems as though the governor views you as a potential enforcer for justice in this skirmish with the Indians."

"I don't recollect ever meeting the governor, but I wouldn't argue with his logic."

"It seems that you've built quite a reputation for hunting men with a price on their heads." He paused to retrieve a bottle from his desk drawer. "Care for a drink, Mr. Quarterman?"

"No thanks. Never touch it."

The colonel poured three fingers into a glass. "These damn Indians seem to think they can oppose the US Government. They've been raiding up and down the river for the past ten days, and they've killed a lot of white settlers." He paused to sip his whiskey. "I've been ordered to stop them by any means, drive them out of the state or put them in the ground. Either way, Ramsey wants them gone. Every last one of 'em."

"Seems like you got enough men right here to get the job done. Just exactly what would you want me for?"

"The governor wants you to use your substantial talents for hunting men as a bounty hunter for the state. He intends to place a cash bounty on every Dakota scalp you can collect."

Arnold stood in amazement, unable to fathom the full meaning of what he had just heard. "You intend to offer a bounty for an Indian scalp? That sounds a bit extreme, if you ask me."

"No one asked you. Extreme, you think? Not if you've seen some of the murdered settlers. I've been in this country for a long time, and believe me, the sooner we deal with these savages, the better."

"Well now, just what kinda bounty are we talking here?"

"We're talking a substantial number. That is if you can live long enough to collect."

"Give me a number. If it's a good one, I'm your man. If it's not, I'll be out of your hair and on my way."

"How does two hundred per scalp strike you? For now, you bring them straight to me. I'll pay you directly soon as you deliver. If I'm in the field, find me. I've been told to always carry enough payroll to settle any debt you bring in."

The deal concluded, and reasoning that most of the fighting was underway north of the Minnesota River, Arnold decided he would focus on stragglers itching to get into the action.

His first encounter took place within hours of leaving Sibley at Fort Ridgley. Negotiating a stream crossing and climbing the ridge on the far side, he found himself face-to-face with a small group of Sioux traveling toward the fort. With only yards between them, surprise and indecision caused him to stop in his tracks. Too close to spin his horse and hightail it to a safer vantage point, he reined in as they continued to close the distance.

His mind cleared as the shock of the encounter vanished, and his instincts took hold. He counted four braves followed by two women walking a horse, a pole flanking each side and secured to the animal with a harness made with rawhide strips. A sapling lashed in place separated the dragging ends of the poles, and the contrivance was webbed with closely intersecting lacings upon which several hide bundles were tied. Following the procession were three mangy dogs. Within moments, the riders drew alongside, and Arnold had no alternative but to face them, expecting the worst.

The men were naked from the waist up; deer hide leggings and moccasins covered the lower half of their bodies. The women had shawls around their necks, crossing in front, covering their breasts, and tied behind their backs. They appeared to be a family moving to a new camp. Sizing up the men, he realized that only three of them capable of putting up a fight—the father and two teenaged boys. The fourth male was not armed and appeared to be no more than twelve years old.

As they drew alongside, Arnold spoke.

"Damn hot day. You'll be heading into a hornet's nest if you keep in the direction you're headed."

The men, initially suspicious of the unexpected rider, relaxed their posture as he spoke. "We're heading east, figuring to pick up the creek and move south, away from the trouble. We got no mind to enter into the fighting."

Arnold, in spite of the August heat, wore the customary fringed leather jacket that had become his trademark. He wore it because it draped over his small frame and gave him the appearance of being larger bodied, giving him a boost of confidence. It also covered the revolver he kept tucked into the waistband of his trousers.

"You best get it done fast. A man named Sibley has a militia garrisoned at Fort Ridgley, and they're itching to get into it." As he spoke, Arnold raised the right side of his jacket to scratch an apparent itch.

The Indian replied, "Obliged for the information. The direction you're going ain't no safer. There are lots of troublemakers moving in from the west." The family began to resume their trek.

Arnold reached to his belt and drew the revolver. At nearly point-blank range, he cocked the hammer, pointed at the older man's chest, and squeezed off a round, sending him cartwheeling to the ground. In quick order, he dispatched the second and third before they could react. With a frenzied intoxication, he turned, wild-eyed, to the remainder of the party, his mind saturated with the power washing over him. Leaning forward, he thumbed the hammer and pointed it at the forehead of the closest woman. The fear in her eyes snapped him back to reality. Lowering his arm, he snarled, "You get on. Take them young'uns and get outta here."

After they disappeared down the slope to the creek, Arnold dismounted and, feeling the euphoria accompanying the taking of a life, collected his first three Dakota scalps.

Feeling that good fortune was with him, he decided to verify the legitimacy of Sibley's claim. Stashing the scalps in one of the saddlebags, he mounted and retraced his steps back to the fort.

* * *

"It didn't take you long to collect them scalps." Sibley was standing outside his office. "Can't be more than six hours since you set out. What's the story on these three?"

"Ain't no never mind. You told me no questions asked, just bring 'em in and collect what I'm owed."

"True enough. Just a little surprising, you bringing in three in such little time."

"I'll tell you how I happened on these here, but it's the last time if you expect me to continue this business."

Sibley stood immobile without saying a word.

"I was riding southwest, and I saw the dust from several ponies kicking up a ways distant. It gave me time to dismount and set up a position to catch them before they spotted me. The three of 'em were riding hard to get to where they was heading, all of 'em painted for war. They even had their horses decked out with mane feathers and paint."

Sibley, clearly in awe, was hanging on every word, and Arnold warmed to his tale.

"I dropped the first one about eighty yards out. The other two came at me screaming and yelling; making enough noise to raise the dead. I took the second with my sidearm moments before they were on me. The third I took with my sidearm as he was about to split my head open with his tomahawk."

"It seems that Alexander Ramsey heard right about you. Shit, man, you keep this up and I'll have to make sure I got a lot of pay at my disposal."

Moments later, Arnold was stoic as he faced the desk of Colonel Henry Hastings Sibley for the second time that day. He watched as the man counted out six hundred dollars in script and handed it to him.

"If you ever get tired of hunting for bounty, look me up. I figure I can always find room in my command for someone with your talents."

The words had imbedded themselves in Arnold's mind.

* * *

Star Woman awoke with a start. Dawn was breaking. She looked around the makeshift camp, amazed that she had slept the night through without so much as changing position. The other three were each as one with the base of the boulder and were still sound asleep, completely unaware that the fire was now nothing more than a heap of hot coals.

She rose to add logs to the bed of glowing coals, and when the others opened their eyes, they were greeted with warm flames.

"It's about time you lazy heads open those eyes. It looks to be a beautiful day, and we've got a long way to go."

Amongst grunts and yawns, the three men emerged from their cocoons, preparing mentally for whatever the day might offer.

The four of them were in fine spirits as they broke camp.

They rode abreast of one another as soon as they reached the level prairie, each of them deep in their own thoughts.

Four Wings, twenty-eight-year-old son of Star Woman, was the first to speak.

"You ever been to these hills we're heading for, Tatemina?"

"Sure have. My father, a cousin, and me rode there in '07. I was just a kid, barely more'n a papoose. I figure I was . . ." a long pause ensued while he calculated on his fingers, "I figure I was around ten years old, or something close to that."

Like Star Woman and Four Wings, Tatemina was Dakota Sioux. Older than the others, at sixty-five years he still possessed considerable skill and had the respect of the others. Before the 1862 war, he was a lead man in a Wahpeton band of Dakota Sioux, and he had participated in more than one treaty signing.

"What's it like?" Four Wings continued. "The hills, I mean."

"You mean the hills themselves?" He paused momentarily. "When we approach, they look black compared to the surrounding land. They just come up out of nowhere; black and beautiful, rising out of the prairie."

"What makes them black?"

"As you get closer, you notice that it's the pines, so thick and heavy with shadow they take on the appearance of being black. It's a beautiful place, a sacred place."

He reached forward to pull remnants of sage weed from his horse's mane, running his fingers through it to remove the tangle.

"When I was there as a young man, there was more game than a man could kill in his lifetime. The black hills are filled with high ridges ringed with forests that hold the deer and elk while the land falls away to create grassy plateaus and beautiful valleys where the bison and turkey thrive."

Four Wings listened with rapt attention. "What of the story that the Black Hills are the source of the Dakota people?"

"Many believe the legend. It tells us that in the time of the ancients, there was one land base and one ocean. They fought terrible wars, and they began to hurt the earth. To stop them, she began to shake, and the land divided into separate islands to isolate the people and stop the destruction brought on by them."

Anton and Star Woman nudged their horses and rode closer to hear what Tatemina was telling the younger man.

He continued, "The people on this island grew as one, but as time passed, they began fighting again and hurting Mother Earth. She sent out warnings to stop, but they didn't listen.

"This time when she shook, the land opened and swallowed, holding the people inside her. After much time, a trickster took the appearance of a white buffalo to lure the people back to the surface."

Tatemina leaned forward and patted the neck of his stallion. "The place of their return is the Black Hills, where they became Oceti Sakowan—The Seven Fires. They are our ancestors, Oyate—The People."

CHAPTER TWO

Spotted Elk

Late January 1863

The four walked their horses. They had skirted the badlands on the northern edge and were now into the hills themselves. The mere presence of the trees, and the absence of the prairie wind, warmed the air. They followed a natural trail that weaved its way up the incline and promised to bring them deeper into the beautiful hills. After continuing for several hours, they stopped to drink and water the horses from a flowing creek.

"This is very different than the Minnesota River basin that we called home." Anton was comfortably seated, leaning against the trunk of a huge pine. "This is beautiful country."

Tatemina was sitting on the opposite side of the same pine, and Four Wings was with the horses as they drank a dozen yards distant. "This is truly a beautiful place," Tatemina agreed. "Star Woman is very strong; she does not need to rest as the men need to rest. Where has she gone?"

Anton looked in the direction she had walked. "She walks to the crest of this hill to get a lay of the land. She is indeed tireless."

The three of them were quiet, the two older men satisfied with reflecting on the day while Four Wings, in apparent boredom, groomed his mount, combing her mane with his fingers.

* * *

She approached as a hunter would stalk a game animal, avoiding sticks, totally silent. When she spoke, all three men were startled, jolted into awareness of her presence.

"There is a camp with three tipis in a depression on the other side of this hill. I watched for a while but saw no movement. Let us move to where we can see them, and we will decide what to do."

Without hesitation, she stepped to her horse, took the reins, and headed for the top of the hill as the men followed. As they were about to crest the top, she stopped, and the men joined her to assess what lay ahead.

She turned to Anton. "It is best that I go in alone. The warriors are not there, and my approach will not threaten those within."

"I think that is not a good idea, Mother," Four Wings interjected.

"Hear me, my son. I will approach alone. You three stay here until I summon you. Tatemina, you have likely done this more than once. You understand the approach of another camp. Those within are surely anxious after what happened in Minnesota and the Mankato hangings. Don't think that word has not spread this far. I suggest the three of you remain out of sight until you are invited."

Star Woman walked with confidence as she advanced toward the small congregation of tipis. Smoke curling from the top told her the one she had to approach.

"Hello inside, my name is Star Woman. I am Dakota. May I speak?"

There was no response, though she could hear movement beyond the flap.

She continued, "I have three friends in the trees to the east. We wish no harm. I am unarmed. My friends hold the horse I rode. We did not want to startle you."

From inside, a voice said, "From what band do you come?"

"My name is Star Woman, and I come from the place of the hangings to the east. I am from the Wahpeton band, that of Red Iron."

The entry flap was pushed aside, and a woman, slightly younger than Star Woman, carefully peeked from the opening. "Come ahead. Have your men remain where they are; you may enter."

Star Woman stooped and entered the structure. Inside were three other young women, a much older woman, and a child. The flap was closed behind her, and she was told to sit. Two of the three women held knives. She folded her legs and sat.

The old lady placed a log on the small fire in the center of the space followed by pine boughs that crackled and popped while thick smoke swirled upward and out the top.

"What is it that you want here?" The old woman was stronger than she first appeared. She approached Star Woman holding a saber of the type carried by cavalry officers. "Why would I not kill you where you sit?"

"Because that would be a mistake. I have no desire to fight you. I come in peace. We have been on the trail for many days. We are cold. We are hungry. We saw your camp. It is simple, we merely . . ."

She moved with unnatural quickness, catching the old woman by surprise, taking her feet out from under her as she swept her leg to make contact. Before the old lady hit the ground, Star Woman was upon her, snatching the saber from her hand as the two younger women looked on with uncomprehending stares.

"Shall we start over?" Star Woman had regained her feet, straddling the old lady; the tip of the saber was inches from the old woman's midsection. "I am not a threat to you. We were hoping for the warmth of your shelter and nothing more."

* * *

"She's been in there for a long time. Do you think we should go on in and make sure she is all right?" Four Wings had been on edge since his mother entered the tipi, and the thick smoke that emanated from the top did nothing to put his mind at ease.

Anton replied, "She's all right. If there was anything she couldn't handle, believe me, that shelter would be on the ground by now. I figure she's just setting the stage for us to make our grand entrance." He leaned his back against one of the aspens comprising the grove in which they waited and prepared to slide to the ground and the blanket he had placed there earlier.

The arrow hit with a solid thump inches above his head. Caught in the unusual position of sliding against the tree, he was unable to do anything except continue toward the ground. Another arrow kicked frozen earth from the ground to his right while a third buried in a fallen aspen to his left.

"Do not move if you value your lives."

The command came from their left. Anton moved his eyes in the direction of the voice as four warriors emerged from the thick stand of trees.

The man speaking wore a bearskin robe that covered his entire body, leather leggings, and substantial hybrid moccasins that were laced nearly to his knees. "Who are you and why have you come? Why are you spying upon our camp?"

Tatemina spoke, "We are not spying. We have come from the Minnesota River Valley. We are Santee. We only wish to find a place where we are welcome."

"We have seen others that came from that place. Some are peaceful, some stir trouble, and yet there are those who seek only to escape the whites. Tell me, which of these are you three?"

"We have another, a different reason for being here. We wish to settle in your beautiful hills and live as Dakota—the life the white man has taken from us."

"Why is it you spy on our camp?"

Anton replied, "We are not spying. My woman is inside your tipi. We wished to cause no surprise. She went in alone so as not to threaten those within. She has been there for some time."

"You will not see her come out. You should hope she is still alive. Those within the shelter are well schooled in protecting what is theirs."

Anton looked in the direction of the encampment. The heavy smoke emitting from the tipi had diminished, and the camp appeared peaceful. He turned toward the man in the bearskin.

"We will not stay where we are not welcome. Tell your men to stand down and allow us passage. There will be no trouble." He again turned to the distant tipi. "I have no fear for my woman; she is very resourceful."

"We will go as one into the camp." The leader motioned to his men, and they lowered their weapons. The party moved toward the tipi. Drawing near, the leader edged to the entry flap and said in a loud voice, "Show us the woman that you hold captive."

There was a stir from inside, the flap was thrown back, and Star Woman appeared in the opening. "Come ahead. We have a strong broth to warm your stomachs and soothe your hunger."

The man in the bearskin robe registered surprise and took a step back.

Star Woman continued, "You are Spotted Elk, who is known in all Dakota Territory as a man of peace."

* * *

The four were invited to spend the night in Spotted Elk's camp, to which they readily agreed. Their time on the trail and the constant riding into the gusting winds of the last few days had tired them to near exhaustion, and this was an opportunity to regain their vigor. They learned that the small group consisted of Spotted Elk, his wife, Walks On Leaves, and members of their family. The others had retired to their shelters.

"I must be getting old, and my hearing suffers," Anton said, "because you were able to approach so close to us without our knowledge."

Walks On Leaves answered for her husband. "Of course. They knew you were in the trees; they had only to learn your exact location before approaching."

"How is it possible that they knew we were watching your camp?"

"Because I told them. We have many ways of warning when danger may be near." She poked at the fire, placed two small pieces of deadwood in its center, and watched them catch the flame. "My son and the others were close by searching for small game for our evening meal. We were here awaiting their return. When Star Woman approached and she told us you were with her, I signaled with smoke that there was danger around the camp. Green wood and pine boughs make much smoke. It was not difficult for Spotted Elk to locate you and approach unnoticed. As you know, stealth is what keeps us fed and alive."

Feeling a bit foolish for being taken off-guard earlier, Anton merely nodded.

"Please ride with us to rejoin our band. We are with Lone Horn. He is a wise leader with many victories. He will welcome you to spend the winter in his camp. It is a day's ride north, into the hills."

So it was settled: Anton, Star Woman, Four Wings, and Tatemina would find sanctuary in the Black Hills of the Dakota Territory.

* * *

Spotted Elk and Walks On Leaves led Star Woman and her entourage along the edge of a precipice. The narrow trail rounded an abutment—a vertical cliff that went straight up a good forty feet before nothing was visible except the sky beyond. Anton figured it leveled off into a broad plateau. To their left was a drop of twice the distance, the bottom of which had a stream that followed the terrain as it weaved its way toward a stand of dark pines.

After navigating their way around the cliff, the path widened into what appeared to be a box canyon surrounded by sheer rock walls.

Four wings turned to Tatemina and whispered, "They have brought us into a dangerous place." They had reached a dead end; the only way out was the way they had entered.

No sooner had he uttered those words than three braves appeared a stone's throw in front of them, effectively blocking their path.

Spotted Elk stopped and turned to the others, "I will see what this is about. You wait here. They will see you as friends while Walks On Leaves is with you."

With that, he put his heels to his mount and cantered toward what were now five braves. Anton watched as his new friend approached the others and entered into a conversation.

Walks On Leaves said, "Spotted Elk is the eldest son of our chief, Lone Horn. These braves are sentries to guard the entrance to the winter encampment. We have had trouble with the Crow, and we must guard against them."

Anton watched as Spotted Elk wheeled his mount and returned to the small group led by Walks On Leaves.

"There have been Crow warriors in the area. The people are cautious, but we may enter."

Anton was searching their surroundings, aware that there was no apparent way to get out of the steep-walled, dead-end canyon they had entered. *We are walking toward a solid rock wall; there is no camp here.* Looking again in the direction of those in front of him, it seemed as if each of them, in turn, disappeared into the wall.

It wasn't until he approached the point where the others had vanished that a narrow crevasse appeared, barely wide enough to allow a horse to pass. Entering the fissure, he advanced a good hundred feet before it turned and began to widen, finally opening and revealing a beautiful landscape fully enclosed within the surrounding granite walls of the adjacent mountains.

They were on the southwest side of the concealed valley, and they followed the trail as it wound from the solid rock through which they had passed, through pockets of cactus and low growth yucca, as they descended toward the valley floor. The transformation from winter to spring was instantaneous.

The sunbeams reflecting off the north face served to warm the hidden oasis in spite of their low angle. The absence of any wind allowed the temperature to climb at least fifty degrees higher than that outside the canyon. A flowing stream snaked along the far side, giving the impression of a dream landscape, one of imagination and totally foreign to the forces outside the proctetive walls.

CHAPTER THREE

The Camp of Lone Horn

Black Hills, Dakota Territory
1863

Anton and Four Wings began to accompany hunting parties to provide fresh meat for the band while Star Woman kept camp and visited with the other women. Tatemina found enjoyment sitting for hours with the older Miniconjou men, talking about the war along the river, perfectly content to let the younger braves hunt for food.

There was much talk among the young warriors in Lone Horn's band in anticipation of the buffalo's reappearance on the northern plains. The opinion of most was that the warm weather of April and the near perfect amount of rain to green the countryside would hasten their return. Anton had never hunted the beasts since most had been pushed west during his formative years in Minnesota Territory. Everything Four Wings knew about them was gleaned from Tatemina, who had hunted them while they still roamed the prairies in the eastern part of the Northwest Territory before they were pushed west.

"Campfire Woman has told me they expect the return of the buffalo very soon," Star Woman said. Campfire Woman was a wife of Spotted Owl, elder Medicine Man for the small band.

"I have heard talk of this for the past several days," Anton replied, looking up from the task at hand. He was working a piece of antler to act as an insert to the grip of a bow he intended as a gift to Spotted Elk for his many kindnesses. He and Star Woman enjoyed the evenings in this Miniconjou camp, and a gift to their benefactor was in order. "I have heard many tales related to the hunt. It would be good if Four Wings and I could participate."

"Have you noticed a change in Four Wings recently?" The casual way in which she asked the question captured his attention. It was not normal for Star Woman to ask questions of her husband; rather, it was her way to speak with respectful authority. She had never questioned the actions of Four Wings in the past unless worry played a part.

Anton looked at her, expecting her face to reveal a hint of the meaning of her question. Her eyes were fixed on the pliable elk pelt she was fashioning into moccasins for her son, and she seemed to be completely absorbed in the task.

"What is it that troubles you about your son?"

She continued to work the leather, appearing to give it her full concentration. "Oh, there is nothing that troubles me." She laced a single, thinly cut strip of rawhide to begin sewing the thicker leather intended for the moccasin sole to the thinner top. "I just wondered if you thought he was acting different somehow."

Anton was at a loss, not having the faintest idea of how to respond. Abruptly, she uttered a barely audible grunt and let her hands fall to her lap.

"I think he is interested in Eagle Feather Man's daughter."

"Woman . . . you scared the daylights out of me. I thought there was something wrong."

"There is something wrong." There was a long pause. "Well, maybe not something wrong, but something different."

They had exposed the reason for Star Woman's troubled mind, and it led them into a discussion that lasted well into the night. The result was inevitable, although hard-won: the leisure time in Lone Horn's camp had given Four Wings the opportunity to find his future—in the form of a woman he intended to have for his wife. It was difficult for Star Woman to accept the thought of stepping away to give her son room to grow, but her intellect told her it had to be done.

The woman at the heart of the matter was the only daughter of Eagle Feather Man, a prominent member of Lone Horn's band. Eagle Feather Man had nine children, all of whom were sons, with a single exception. The firstborn was a daughter considered to be the most beautiful in the band of Lone Horn's Miniconjou Teton Sioux. Her name was Gentle Breeze, and although many had tried to win her, Eagle Feather Man turned out to be as protective of her as he was of anything he possessed. There had not been a suitor considered qualified to take her away, and her father's requirements had been impossible to satisfy.

This was a fact not lost on Four Wings, nor on Anton, Star Woman, or Tatemina, nor on every member of Lone Horn's band.

She would be a hard-won prize indeed.

* * *

"The buffalo have returned!" The scout galloped through the camp. "The buffalo have returned! The Great Spirit has brought them back to us."

Murmurs turned to shouts of joy as word spread among the people. Young men urged going forth to begin the hunt, while those with more seasons behind them sought to postpone the action until a solid plan was devised to ensure the best results possible.

Lone Horn gathered his men, and a conference was held. The hunt would commence only after ensuring the participation of the entire band. The return of the buffalo meant the abandonment of their winter camp; much planning was necessary.

It took all of the next day for them to prepare to strike their camp and move their possessions outside the wintering valley to embark on the summer season of moving wherever the buffalo took them. Two days later they were near the herd and ready to begin the hunt.

The youngest men would be drivers to move the buffalo toward a designated point; the ablest would ride their horses into the herd, shooting arrows from point-blank range into the hearts of the beasts while racing alongside at breakneck speeds. The old men, women, and children would follow on foot, reaping the rewards provided by the Great Spirit for their continued good fortune. Theirs was the task of ensuring that nothing of the animal was wasted.

It was time for the Dakota Sioux to learn the hunt from their Lakota brothers and sisters.

Encountering a stretch of open grassland within the hills, they found a herd of over a thousand of the massive animals, and the hunt began. With a whoop, the riders swept toward the buffalo, driving them south while mounted warriors charged the fringes of the fleeing herd. Four Wings could do no more than watch in amazement as creature after creature stumbled and fell, mortally wounded by the accurate placement of arrows by those riding like madmen alongside the beasts.

He watched one of the riders somersault from the back of his pony as it caught a hoof on a deadfall half-buried in the meadow grass. Without hesitation, Four Wings urged his mare forward.

The stampeding mass seemed to pulse, expanding and contracting as it flowed across the valley. The brave who had fallen happened to be in the center of a void within the pulsing herd. Four Wings knew the opening would close, and the Indian would be trampled unless he could reach him in time. The distance he had to cover would require him to sweep into a natural swale if he was to arrive in time to save the man's life.

Hugging low on his horse's neck, he flattened himself and urged her to greater and greater speed.

The massive herd had begun to swing in the direction of the downed man. The warrior saw the approaching animals and knew his life was about to end. Showing extreme courage, he stood his ground and watched as the lead bull came into focus with a clarity the man had never seen before; coal-black eyes were set in a massive face that was topped with two curved horns as white as snow, and dust blew from his nostrils. The warrior had begun his death song when a lone rider seemed to erupt from the very ground to his left.

Four Wings emerged from the swale at a gallop, face obstructed by the mare's flailing mane as he remained close to her body. Closing the distance, mere yards ahead of the charging herd, he grabbed a handful of the mane, lowered his arm, and rode for the warrior on the ground.

As though they had rehearsed it many times, the grounded brave hooked Four Wings's extended arm and swung upward unto the horse's back. His arms wrapped around his rescuer's torso, the two men raced out of danger from the approaching beasts.

Once in the clear, the two of them swung to the ground and watched as the old men, women, and children walked the now trampled earth, stopping at each carcass to begin the task of skinning and processing the animals into much-needed food and supplies. Not a single remnant of the beasts remained unclaimed.

As it happened, the young warrior Four Wings rescued was named Many Feathers, son of Eagle Feather Man. Upon hearing of the bravery of the Dakota warrior living in their midst, Eagle Feather Man hosted a buffalo dance in celebration. The men that had exhibited special bravery during the hunt carried buffalo horns and made their way among the dancers, who were winding their way around the central fire, bobbing and weaving as the men with the horns passed them by. Although many brave deeds had been performed during the hunt, none were as noteworthy as that accomplished by Four Wings when he saved Eagle Feather Man's son.

The warrior who showed the greatest bravery during the hunt was awarded a full buffalo cape and, as tradition mandated, bumped the dancers that came within reach. Four Wings was honored with the cape.

It did not go unnoticed by Star Woman that the caped buffalo seemed to favor bumping the beautiful Gentle Breeze every time they passed.

CHAPTER FOUR

Sibley's Minnesota Quarters

June 1863

"**G**ood seeing you again, little man."

Arnold bristled at the comment. "Listen, Colonel, I ever hear you call me that again, it'll be the last time you see me. Ain't no call to refer to me that way."

"I meant no disrespect; in fact, just the opposite. I've never seen anybody who can do what you can." Sibley was taken aback by Arnold's reaction and unfamiliar with being talked to in such a manner. "It won't happen again."

Their eyes locked, and Arnold knew he had nearly crossed a line. This man was used to wielding his power. Tense and ready to explode, he calmed himself. He knew it was a shortcoming, but he couldn't help it. His height, or rather his lack of height, had a profound effect on his life, and he hated some of the names he had been called in his early years.

"Sorry, Colonel. I guess I been fighting that for a long time."

Sibley was curt. "Have you considered the proposal I made the last time we met?"

There was a long pause before he answered. "I'm willing to give it a try." There was another long pause before he continued. "I ain't interested in enlisting, so if that's a requirement, forget it. I'd be interested as long as it's a job; one I can quit if it turns into something I get my fill of and decide to leave."

"I can live with that arrangement. I can pay you cash money once a month right out of the bounty money supplied by Governor Ramsey. I'd just as soon keep it between us, no sense in having it go any further. We're planning an expedition into Dakota Territory to keep these bastards on the move and take out all we can. I sure could use your expertise. I could give you command of twenty or thirty men, all handpicked by you. You'd pick up an officer's pay, plus your food, horse, and everything that goes with it. You'd be billeted same as the other officers, which is a damn sight better than the enlisted men."

As Arnold listened, excitement began to build. Sibley continued, "Best of all, you won't be alone. You'll have the US Army to back you up."

"Colonel, I got another request."

Sibley stood and walked to the window overlooking the fort's parade grounds. "I'd advise you not to push your luck. The offer stands as delivered. Take it or leave it."

"Colonel, I need rifles for me and the men I select. It's damn important if you expect me to do what you want done. That's what I need. The latest rifles the army has. I'm looking for repeating rifles and as much ammunition as we need for training and field work."

Arnold was pleased to see Henry Sibley nod his head in agreement.

* * *

Dakota Territory

Henry Sibley, now with the brevet rank of brigadier-general of volunteers, was leading his force of over three thousand men in pursuit of the escaping Sioux who had moved west after their defeat at the Battle of Wood Lake along the Minnesota River basin. Riding at Sibley's side was Arnold Quarterman.

As agreed, Arnold had chosen twenty men to train for their task. Arnold's choice of personnel was likely the most unusual ever assembled as a fighting unit in the US Army. In addition to proven above-average athletic skills and lean, muscular bodies, each man was no taller than five foot six. Stealth was paramount to success.

The final piece necessary for successful completion of their mission was the rifle the men would carry.

In his hands, Arnold held Sibley's contribution to his armory, a Spencer .52 caliber, breechloading, lever-action repeating rifle. He felt an initial disappointment with the choice after owning his Henry repeating rifle, which had a faster rate of fire. After practicing with the Spencer, he considered the new rifle a step up due to its long-range accuracy. The only drawback to the Spencer was that after levering a new bullet into the chamber, it required manually cocking the hammer for each firing. But with a rate of fire of fourteen to twenty rounds per minute, the Spencer would be sufficient. Arnold had a new favorite weapon.

His assignment was to lead his small detachment as an advance unit to surprise Indian encampments discovered by the scouts.

Gathering his small contingent of men, Arnold explained their mission. "Okay, Long Rifles. We are the tip of the sword, the catalyst that will break the resolve of the Indian." He stood on the empty munitions crate that was now a standard part of his retinue; at eighteen inches deep, he found that when turned upside down it elevated his physical presence above those he addressed. The crate was Arnold's equalizer.

A large part of making the plan feasible would be the ability of the sharpshooters to establish a position without being noticed. Their opening volley would be a complete surprise. "As long as we are on the trail, we will practice with these rifles. When we're not shooting, you will be learning to conceal yourselves. Being able to hide is what's gonna keep you alive."

Training began with learning the proper use of the rifle, making every shot the result of careful aiming before squeezing the trigger. It wasn't long before his recruits were hitting a five-inch circle at fifty-yards with fewer than two seconds between shots.

The issue of gaining position without being noticed, and effective concealment after settling in, turned out to be the most difficult to master. Skilled in concealment and ruthless cunning, Arnold trained his troops to control their instincts and settle in as one with the land, the very skills that had made him a success as a bounty hunter. And he reveled in the power he possessed.

By the third week of training, Arnold was leading his men on field exercises, and he loved every moment. They began by leaving the overnight camps long before dawn and setting up an ambush for the main party. Their distance from the passing troops had to be within the limits of their ability to fire a lethal round. If they remained undetected by the entire command as it passed their location, their exercise was considered successful.

Arnold's men were being trained to spread themselves over a wide area to make them appear as a much larger force. They were trained in a technique to stagger their shots in a manner that allowed a constant barrage from the entire width of men.

These were thrilling times, and Arnold loved the action. While he took advantage of every situation, the single most critical factor in his mind was the control he had over the men he was training. He excelled in wielding his illegitimate yet newfound power, demanding perfection from his men.

* * *

The fleeing Dakota families, led by Standing Buffalo and protected by the war chief Inkpaduta, also known as Scarlet Point, had stopped to allow the women and children to rest. Standing Buffalo had been on the trail for over a month with the intent of bringing his people north into Canada to escape the white army intent on hunting them down.

On July 24, Sibley's force of thirty-three hundred men caught them at their encampment at a place called Big Mound, taking them completely by surprise, Arnold's men performed impressively, killing many and allowing Sibley to charge into the large camp nearly uncontested, where many Indians were cut down and their supplies destroyed.

Sibley's men had been on the march for thirty days, and they were tired and angry. Inkpaduta had fought a delaying action, stalling their advance on the escaping Indians, and the men were frustrated.

"You there . . . you—Trooper," Sibley snapped. "Ride along the line and tell Colonel McPhail that I need him here."

Within two minutes, McPhail reined in at Sibley's left side, opposite Arnold on the right.

"The scouts tell me there's a lake ahead," Sibley said. "I need you to bring the men closer together. Tighten up the ranks and move about forty men behind those mule carts. We'll set camp alongside the lake to give the men a break and let the stock graze."

"Yes, sir." McPhail put his heels to his horse's flanks and rode back along the line of men, heading for the trailing pack train.

The lake they were approaching was surrounded by uneven terrain; rolling hills separated by mostly gentle yet sometimes steep-walled draws. Fixing on a spot suitable for a bivouac, Sibley dismounted and waited for his command to gather. He turned to Arnold. "We'll settle in here for a time and catch some well-earned rest. Have you got your men ready to go? I have a feeling that action isn't far off. Best make sure the troops are ready when I need 'em."

"They'll be ready, General."

Arnold turned his horse and muttered under his breath, "Stupid bastard, of course they're ready." He rode off in the direction where the Long Rifles, a name he now thought perfectly suited them, were making camp.

Arnold had an acute awareness of the capabilities of the Indians they were following, and while Sibley and the confident officers and troops he commanded seemed intent on setting camp on the shores of the lake, he had noticed the appearance of Indians visible from time to time on the hills ahead.

Gathering his Long Rifles, he addressed them. "Men, stay awake and ready for trouble. I figure Sibley is overconfident and yearning for a good night's sleep. Don't get taken in by this here lull. There's plenty of trouble waiting in them hills ahead, and I figure it'll be coming for us soon enough."

After settling his men into a routine to avoid any surprise attack, he headed for Sibley's tent.

"General, my men are ready if you want us to bring the fight to them what are in the hills. I seen a bunch of 'em moving around up there, and I figure we could move in and catch 'em unawares."

As though he hadn't heard a word, Sibley exited the tent and approached McPhail a short distance away.

"There's plenty of Indians in them hills yonder. Get them cannons up here and give 'em a lesson in long-range warfare. We back 'em up, and we'll get us a good night's sleep."

Arnold watched as the cannons were brought up and begin firing into the surrounding hills. Too reliant upon chance to make a lucky shot, the result was to drive the Indians farther away, out of reach of the guns. A lull ensued. Confidence in their ability to drive the Indians away without as much as a close confrontation took over the encampment.

The packs were removed from the train animals, and several of the mules and horses were set to graze on the tender grasses outlining the small lake. Two sentries were set in place to keep the animals from straying, and the camp settled in for an evening break as troopers washed in the nearby lake and sentries were posted on the outskirts.

* * *

In the Dakota camp, Standing Buffalo and Inkpaduta had been joined by a party of Lakota braves. Knowing of the predicament facing the Dakotas, the Lakota were prepared to protect them until they crossed the Missouri River. One of the leaders of the Lakota was a Hunkpapa chief named Sitting Bull. Earlier, he had called a council with his warriors.

"It is not my wish to kill the whites. If we can take their supplies, they will be crippled, and the fight will be over. They will not continue in pursuit of our Dakota brothers."

Intermixed with the Lakota was a small group of Wahpeton Dakota who had seen friends die along the Minnesota River during the uprising, and they wanted revenge. Wolf Dog Shield spoke on their behalf, "We must avenge our people. This Sibley killed much family last year; we can overrun his camp and have a great victory."

"Yes, we can do that, but to what end?" Sitting Bull argued. "If we kill this Sibley, more will follow. The white men are like the grass; there are more of them than all the tribes together would number." He looked at the faces surrounding him.

"If we fight to control our rightful land, it is one thing; if we fight to kill the white man, it is something else. Have we not seen what happened to our Santee brothers and sisters when they entered into war with the whites? Let us demonstrate our ability as warriors in a way that will earn their respect."

The others were listening, so he continued to press his point.

"We will show them our abilities without killing. We will take their pack animals, and they will turn away."

He prevailed.

A short while later a small group of warriors crept toward the grazing mules. They were nearly invisible as they belly-crawled through the foot-high grasses filling the depressions pocketing the area. Leading them was the Hunkpapa chief, Sitting Bull.

He now approached the grazing mules, accompanied by two others from his band. None of the three carried weapons; the objective was to steal pack animals without being discovered.

There were two troopers stationed as sentries to watch the animals and supplies. Sitting Bull had crawled close enough to hear their conversation while his accomplices advanced a good thirty yards to his right.

"Watcha thinkin' about them Injuns what came in a while ago, Grady? I gotta say them ain't much to fear if'n that's all they got to offer." Samuel Graves was doing his best to be philosophical. "I heard tell that these Sioux is scary fighters. I ain't seen it yet. I figure we whooped 'em a good'n back at Big Mound, and these'uns ain't nothin' to fear."

Grady was in the process of packing his pipe with the last of the tobacco he carried. "Don't you figure you better get yer ass down t'other end of the line and cover them mules, Sam? Bigger'n shit Sibley's likely layin' on a cot, and you sure don't want Colonel McPhail to catch you off yer post."

"I ain't scared of McPhail," Samuel said, though he wasted no time as he hustled to his sentry post a hundred yards to the east.

Sitting Bull heard the exchange and a smile crossed his face. His two companions had spread out to his right, the retreating Samuel passing within a few feet of where they lay in the heavy grass.

Raising his head to see over the tall grass, he saw the only tree on this side of the lake—a red cedar—and it grew very near to where the man named

Grady now stood. In fact, Grady had carelessly leaned his rifle against one of the tree's lower branches.

Looking to his right, Sitting Bull realized his comrades had stopped moving forward and were now focusing their attention on him. Ducking below the tops of the grasses and carefully peeking through openings, he saw that the majority of the grazing animals had moved farther toward the lake, leaving an expanse of open ground between the guards and the animals.

Grady had now gone down on his haunches, arms folded over his knees, intent on smoking his newly lit pipe. It was early afternoon, and the July sun beat down with a ferocious intensity that had the man removing his trooper's hat and wiping his brow with regularity.

Sitting Bull, after studying the area and confirming there was no other enemy close by, gathered himself, bounced into a crouch, and sprinted to the cedar while holding his body as close to the ground as possible, keeping the cedar between him and the sentry, Grady.

Reaching the tree growing in the open, he hugged the ground and became as invisible as a spider in the grassy terrain surrounding the tree.

Grady, oblivious to the warrior not ten feet to his rear, continued to puff on his pipe. The moments passed, and, satisfied that the tobacco had been entirely consumed, he tapped the pipe on a small stone to clear the bowl and began to stand. Something clamped onto his shoulder and prevented him from straightening.

As panic set in, Grady spun to his left and fell to the ground, empty pipe sailing six feet away. In terror, he looked upon the face of Sitting Bull, passive, composed, and with a streak of red traversing from his right forehead to left jowl, making him a fearsome spectacle. Most unnerving of all was that the Indian had his index finger placed vertically against his lips, indicating silence. In his free hand, he held Grady's rifle.

Grady's mind had trouble comprehending the situation. Moments before, he was alone on the open prairie, and his fellow sentry was visiting with him. The next thing he knew, out of nowhere appeared a Sioux warrior with a countenance so fierce it was capable of driving off the devil himself; and the topper—all this warrior did was beckon him to be silent. It was too much. Grady felt the warmth of urine as his bladder emptied.

From the main encampment, shooting erupted. Sitting Bull calmly got to his feet, walked a short ways to the grazing mule, wrapped a rawhide strip around its muzzle, swung unto its back, and galloped from the scene, rifle in hand, as the warriors that had come with him sprinted ahead. What began as a raid to take supplies turned into a show of bravery as Sitting Bull rode the government mule from the army camp after counting coup on one of the guards, an action that would add to his already impressive list of accomplishments.

Sporadic attempts by Inkapudta to probe the drawn out string of army positions looking for a soft spot proved to no avail . Eventually, they withdrew and Standing Buffalo resumed his journey toward the Missouri River, Sibley's forces enjoyed a much-needed rest, and Inkpaduta prepared his men for fighting a rear guard delaying action .

* * *

For the next two weeks, the main party of Sioux stayed ahead of Sibley's command as they moved toward the Missouri River. The whole time, the pursuing army was suffering significant delays caused by the rear guard led by Inkpaduta. His concern for his people and their crossing of the river before being overtaken by Sibley's forces gave him and his warriors the reason to fight and stall Sibley's advance until the main body of people were safely west of the Missouri.

Sibley and his men were exhausted and nearly out of supplies. The men had tired of the prospect of marching into the teeth of the rear guard and had lost the will to fight. They had been on the trail for forty-two days and had fought three significant battles as they chased the Sioux toward the Missouri River. The campaign was drawing to its end. The plan had called for Sibley's troops to link up with troops led by General Alfred Sully with the intent of catching the retreating Sioux in a pincer movement. But Sully failed to show. After a fitful night, Sibley called Arnold into his presence.

Arnold, aware of the general feeling of discord expressed by the troops, was nonetheless surprised at what he heard.

"I'll be heading home in the morning, so I won't be needing your services."

Sibley was sitting on a chair outside his tent. In front of him was a folding table upon which he made his reports and various notes for his commanding officers to be delivered by courier.

The general plopped a canvas pouch on the table and pushed it toward Arnold.

"This here's the rest of the bounty money I brought with me. Not much left, but it's yours. General Sully is heading this way; he should have been here by now. I've got a feeling he can use your particular expertise. He'll be heading to the other side of the river to clean the territory of the Sioux. If you like, I'll send him a message telling him you'll be waiting for him. You can work out whatever you want with him. I figure he's got a few more of these repeating rifles in his command."

On August 12, 1863, Henry Hastings Sibley started the trek homeward. His time of active pursuit of the Indians was over.

The diminutive Arnold Quarterman rode toward Fort Pierre to await the arrival of General Alfred Sully.

* * *

Whatever Sibley had told Sully, it worked to Arnold's advantage. The deal he struck with General Sully was much the same as the one he'd had with Sibley. An advantage was that the riflemen were already expert marksmen. Another difference was that every single one of them was at least eight inches taller than Arnold.

His first reaction was extreme displeasure, but it soon turned to his advantage by filling him with a feeling of emmense power. Such was the result of something called "chain of command." Arnold's position as a leader benefited him because his superior rank guaranteed submission by the men in his command.

Arnold came on strong. "All right, you men belong to me. You will do as I command, or you will return to the nondescript status of an infantry private, and your rifle will be taken by your replacement."

That was enough to guarantee their cooperation, and as time passed they developed the attitude that Arnold garnered within them. Each was superior to the others in Sully's command, and they harbored a strange kinship with the little man that talked like he was a giant.

* * *

Much to General Sully's displeasure, he was ordered to accompany a caravan of settlers and miners heading toward the newly discovered goldfields of eastern Oregon Territory. Sully followed orders but did not disguise his contempt while doing so.

After attacking and destroying a large encampment at a place called Killdeer Mountain, where women and children were targeted and huge amounts of food and supplies were destroyed, Sully entered the northern Dakota badlands. As much as he disliked his orders, he was committed to escorting the train through the badlands to Fort Union on the Missouri River. Fort Union was not a military post, as the name would imply; instead, it was the westernmost trading post on the river, and once there, General Sully would be free of the emigrant encumbrance. Unfortunately, it also meant he needed to close out his campaign and bring his men home before being trapped in place by the winter weather.

During the arduous trek through the badlands, Arnold had been called upon nearly every day to take a number of his men with him and ride ahead of the main party. He was given a guide from the Mandan tribe who knew the badlands very well. Word began to spread among the emigrant train that Arnold was heading the scouting party, and those in the train viewed him as the primary scout. Arnold saw an opportunity to turn his false skills into a profitable venture. Knowing the makeup of the train, he was aware of the group of prospectors that traveled with them. He also knew that they were to spend the winter at the fort.

Seeing the makings of a potential payday in this group of men, he decided to remain at Fort Union through the winter months. He bid General Sully a safe journey and settled in.

A month went by, and Arnold began to question his choice to stay at the fort after Sully took his command east for the winter. Expecting to be approached by the prospectors to serve as their guide to the goldfields, he remained aloof, solitary, not joining the men that came to barter furs for any number of supplies.

Finally reconciling himself with the error of his decision to stay for the winter, he left his room and entered the trading floor, where card games were a staple during the winter months. At one side of the rectangular room was a long bar that served spirits. Making his way to the far end, he stopped and asked for a glass of water; after seeing what alcohol did to other men, he avoided it.

He had barely brought the glass to his lips when he was approached by a man he recognized as one of the prospectors traveling with the train. He had made it his job to learn each of the men's names. A satisfied feeling came over Arnold as the man he knew as Harold Stone joined him at the bar.

Harold was a bull of a man, the kind that excelled at throwing his weight around to impress men with less physical endowments. Arnold had learned that the man was a bully. He had formed a group of like-minded men determined to break away from the main body and travel a more direct route to the goldfields they sought.

"Mr. Quarterman, my name's Stone. I got me twenty-three good and ready men what want to move straight as an arrow to them goldfields. Seems no point in goin' roundabout. We be lookin' for someone to take the point with enough savvy to skirt them Indians and the stones to fight our way through if necessary."

"I don't figure you're gonna find anybody to do that job, at least nobody that wants to save his hair and live to a ripe old age."

"What if I told you we'd pay a handsome price to someone that could get us there?"

"I doubt that even fifty men could come up with enough money to tempt me into doing the job. No doubt I'd deliver, but I just ain't interested in risking my neck, especially after leading General Sully into and out of those badlands."

The truth was that he'd had nothing at all to do with the trek; in fact, he and his men had relied totally on Sully's Mandan Indian scout to point the trail. But the emigrant train only saw what they perceived as an elite unit clearing the way.

"I've been fighting these savages for a long time, Mr. Stone. I doubt you've got enough money to entice me to join you."

"The name's Stone—forget the mister. I'm sorry you feel that way."

"Well, that's the truth of it. I don't know what you were gonna offer, but unless it's a hell of a lot more than I think you can muster, the answer is no. I've got a family waiting for me back in Minnesota." He delivered the lie convincingly. "You can talk to your men and see what you can do, but don't waste my time. There ain't a man anywhere near here that can get you through the Powder River country safely 'cept me."

Arnold turned and walked away. He had laid the groundwork; it was now time to wait and see if he had made a convincing enough performance to generate an offer that he couldn't refuse.

* * *

Three days had passed, and the two men sat as before in the trading post. Harold Stone laid out his offer. Arnold Quarterman sat opposite the table.

"Every wagon has agreed to the sum of fifty dollars for you to get us to the Montana goldfields," Stone opened the negotiation.

Arnold had barely let the words settle when he pushed his chair back and rose to leave. "I thought I made myself clear the last time we talked about this. I got me a family waiting for my return. Fifty dollars per wagon ain't enough for me to delay that return for two weeks, let alone two months. You're wasting my time."

"Now hold on a minute there! Sit your ass down, and let's talk about this."

"Ain't nothing to talk about, Stone. If you need a guide, you're gonna have to look someplace else 'cause that ain't enough to pull me off the shitter, let alone guide a train of greenhorns west." Arnold had found that when dealing with anyone bigger than he was, it was best to talk like he was eight feet tall and indestructible. He had been doing it since he was fifteen, and he was very good at bluster.

"If you can't do any better'n that, I'll just keep walking. If you got money you ain't spent, you better get it out and make me an offer that's worth listening to. We'll do this one more time, and only once, so make me the best you've been authorized to make, or you can blow kisses to my ass as I walk out that door yonder."

43

Thirty minutes later, Arnold Quarterman walked out fifteen hundred dollars richer, with an agreement to guide the train to Virginia City, and another fifteen hundred to be paid when they arrived. Both men knew the folly of trying the trek in the dead of winter, so the agreement to begin in the spring was satisfactory to both parties.

* * *

Arnold Quarterman prepared himself for leading the prospectors to the western Montana goldfields. As a result of his agreement with Stone, Arnold spent the winter seeking and finding men that had been in the Powder River country. His agreement with Stone was that they would move when the weather broke, and the spring thaw was under way. During the long winter, he had been able to mine information from the occasional mountain man, the more occasioned Indians, and the rare but reliable French traders. His mission had been to garner information that would help him locate known routes to the goldfields.

By May, he was ready. Armed with hand-drawn maps from several sources, he combined the information, often totally reliant on his faith in the person providing it, to outweigh discrepancies evident in the rough drawings. It was as much gut feeling and reliance on intellect to separate the wheat from the chaff. If multiple sources indicated a stream crossing at a certain location while others favored crossing miles upstream or downstream, Arnold notched both crossings, with the one he favored marked in a special way.

Arnold had studied his maps over the winter, and with the arrival of spring he was prepared to lead his first line of wagons across the high plains of Montana Territory in a diagonal southwestern direction from Fort Union, between the Missouri and Yellowstone Rivers, over the mountains via a pass told to him by a grizzled trapper he'd met over the winter, then on to Virginia City.

When they left Fort Union, Arnold was in his element. Any time he had command over others, he became inflated with that power to the extent of being repugnant to those under his command. He was in control of men that were physically superior to him. His preparation had been top notch, and he reveled in degrading comments for the unfortunate individual that deviated the least bit from his instructions. After significant berating of men that were twice his size, strictly because he loved to show his authority, and after four days of uneventful travel, he was able to lead the party to the Musselshell River. It was the night of the new moon—the darkest of all the nights of the month—and they had set camp in the late afternoon. The men sought the chilly waters of the river to wash away the grime collected after four days on the trail.

Arnold and Stone sat opposite each other, separated by a low fire. They were removed a distance from the rest of the train. Roasting over the flame was a rabbit Stone had killed as it bolted from cover at the river's edge.

"Damn, we been makin' good time, little man."

"Name's Arnold, you big blowhard. You call me that again, and we'll be going our separate ways."

"Take it easy. I was just makin' small talk and tossing you a compliment."

"I noticed, and the name's still Arnold. I figure we're over halfway, but the toughest part of the trip is just ahead. Before we get to the pass, I'd like to make sure you got the final payment stashed where you can get it."

"Don't you worry about gettin' paid. I got the money, all right."

"You best dig it out and let me see it. There's sign all over says we're in the middle of Indian territory. We're gonna have to move mostly at night to avoid running into them."

Arnold unsheathed his knife and sliced a front leg off the sizzling rabbit. "We get into a skirmish, I want to know where you are to make sure you don't skedaddle."

"Why, you little prick. I oughta give you a good whippin'."

"I figure you could give it a try, but I wouldn't advise it. All's I need is reassurance that you got the money. Another week should get us there. Wouldn't set well if we couldn't settle up on our last night on the trail."

Stone glared at the little man. He had taken all he could take. It was time to beat some respect into the runt. With a menacing scowl, he stood. "It's time you learned a few manners."

From nowhere, a gun appeared in Arnold's hand.

"You better give that a second thought. I won't have any problem at all shooting you in the stomach. Hell of a way to die, I hear."

Stone stopped in his tracks. He had heard how dangerous the man facing him was, and he didn't want to test it.

"Why don't you just tell me where you keep the money, and we'll let it go for now." Arnold continued to point the barrel at the big man.

"I keep it close to me all the time. I use my saddlebag as a pillow for more reason than support. That's where I keep the money; ain't nobody gonna get their fingers on it without me knowing."

Arnold slowly raised the muzzle and squeezed the trigger. The shot caught Stone dead center in the chest, blowing him backward a good four feet. Without hesitation, Arnold stood and fired several times into the darkness.

"Help! You men get over here. We got us an Indian that shot Stone. Get over here—NOW!" He fired again into the night.

Arnold kicked at the fire, sending embers into the sky, adding to the chaos of the moment. As the closest men charged toward the shouting, Arnold dashed to Stone's horse tied to the rear of the wagon, still saddled and waiting to be stripped, curried, and offered her daily dose of grain. Seeing the saddlebags tied securely behind the saddle, he untied the reins and climbed the spokes until he could reach the saddle horn, and swung into the saddle just as the first man from the train cleared the wagon and came into sight.

He wheeled the horse to come alongside the growing group rushing toward the prostrate Stone.

"You men take care of Stone. I'm going to catch that son of a bitch. I hit him with my first shot. He can't go too far. You take care of Stone; I'll be back as soon as I kill that bastard."

As soon as Arnold was out of their sight, he slowed the horse to a walk. *That couldn't have worked out better if I had planned it. After all that noise, every Indian within hearing will know they're there. I wouldn't give a plug nickel for their chances.*

He rode south, crossed the Yellowstone River, and entered into Powder River country. Since his killing of Stone and the exuberant feeling of power that coursed through his body with that act, his mind focused on little else. He spent his days looking for ways to rekindle the innermost pleasure he had felt when the gun recoiled in his hand and the bullet ripped into Stone's body.

He began to long for the exquisite satisfaction he felt when he held the power of life and death over another person and saw the fear in their faces.

In the summer of 1865, Arnold Quarterman began the cold-blooded killing of white settlers and miners moving along the trail. His targets were single wagons, where he could make quick work of the party, search their belongings, taking what he deemed of value, then burn what was left, including the bodies of men, women, and children unlucky enough to have crossed his path.

* * *

The morning promised a clear day as the eastern sky began to lighten. Arnold had reached the top of a predominant hill adjacent to his camp. He figured it would allow him to see a great distance and possibly discover the campsite of a trespasser. It was his job to keep the area free of interlopers. Once at the top, he could see for miles in every direction.

With the collapsing telescope that Sibley had given him, he scanned the area. It was dead calm when he first noticed the narrow plume of smoke rising straight up from the trees at the edge of the swampy land three miles or so distant. He felt the rush of excitement as he watched through the lens and imagined what his immediate future held.

Scrambling down the incline, he ran to his camp and retrieved his rifle from his bedroll and set off in the direction of the trespasser's camp. Familiar with the terrain, he followed a small stream eastward as it descended toward a large swampy area. Once at the swamp, he slowed his approach, knowing his advantage was in stealth. He knew he was close when he spotted hazy smoke drifting between the green boughs twenty feet above.

What we got here is squatters that are gonna learn to stay off my land.

The trees and dense bushes grew almost to the edge of the creek that flowed into the marshy area, where it meandered before joining the main river. A tipi was set in a small clearing to one side. It was approaching noon when he finally moved into position.

The thick bushes were impossible to penetrate, so Arnold had resorted to wading in the shallows as he made his way around a large willow growing on the edge of the creek. Moving carefully to avoid making any noise, he spread the reeds to get his bearings.

As he looked through the part in the reeds, there, staring him square in the face, was a woman. Startled, he took a step backward, catching his heel on a submerged branch, sending him tumbling backward into the water. The woman, also surprised at the sight of a white man inches from her face, was momentarily frozen in place, unable to move from her position. Finally, realization struck home, and she turned to run. Unfortunately for her, Arnold had also recovered, lifted his rifle, and shot her before she could leave the dense grass at the edge of the stream.

A warrior stepped out of the tipi, and Arnold swung his rifle and fired, driving the man back into the shelter. In less than a minute, it was over.

Arnold looked from side to side as an understanding of what had just happened settled in his mind. There was no sound. The frogs and birds had gone silent, and the usual sounds of bugs and swaying grasses and leaves inherent on a summer day had vanished. Fearing that he had gone deaf, he moved his feet along the creek bottom, releasing the sound of the river as it poured over the rocks and among the cattails and reeds lining the shore.

Hot damn! Weren't that somethin'! Arnold, eyes wide as he climbed from the water, was overtaken with the feeling of power. *Let's see what we got us.*

He moved quickly to the open flap and cautiously peeked inside. There lay the brave; the shot had torn through his midsection, clipping a main artery. Surrounded by a pool of blood, Arnold figured he had died within a minute or two. Taking his knife, he swept it across the man's stomach, tumbling his innards to the ground.

He moved to the water, cut several heavy reeds, and brought them back to the tipi. He proceeded to stir them in the warrior's blood and begin to print on the outside walls of the tipi. When he finished, he stood back to admire his work: STAY OFF MY LAND.

Satisfied, he kneeled at the man's side and cut across his forehead. As if he were skinning a beaver, he removed the scalp, then backed out into the open, closed the tipi flap, and turned toward the creek. Repeating the process on the woman, he held both scalps in his left hand and snapped to attention, delivering a proper salute with his right.

"Altogether now, men." With a flourish, he raised his hands as a music conductor directing a band and began to sing, in a loud voice rippling with patriotism, one of the two songs he knew.

"O, I wish I was in the land of cotton,

Old times there are not forgotten,

Look away, look away, look away, Dixie Land."

CHAPTER FIVE

The Eagle

Since the celebration of the buffalo hunt, Gentle Breeze had spent considerable time in the company of Star Woman. It was no secret that she cast an approving eye upon Four Wings, and he let it be known that she was someone he viewed as special. The rules surrounding the process of wooing a woman were well known, as was Eagle Feather Man's reputation for being overprotective. Without his approval, there would be no physical contact between his daughter and a potential suitor, and though many had sought his permission, all had fallen short.

And so now Four Wings sat across from Eagle Feather Man, the fire Eagle Feather Man had started the previous evening between them. Although the autumn weather was warm, he was a man that trusted family tradition, and tradition said if a suitor was expected to appear, the fire would tell if he was worthy. It had worked many times when lesser braves had come calling on his daughter and had been found wanting.

Four Wings began, "I have come to ask permission to seek favor with your daughter."

Eagle Feather Man showed no emotion, sitting immobile, eyes fixed on the glowing embers between them. He sat that way for many minutes, and with each passing moment, Four Wings became more and more anxious.

Finally, Eagle Feather Man spoke, "Replenish the fire, and we shall talk."

"May I go for wood, that your fire shall be one of beauty and much heat?"

"You may."

Four Wings slowly got to his feet and backed from the tipi. As soon as he was outside, he hurried to gather deadwood scattered beneath the assortment of trees near the temporary camp. He reasoned he needed a quick, easily ignited source to pass the flame to more substantial fuel.

Within a short time, he was headed back to Eagle Feather Man's tipi.

"What have you brought to the fire?"

"I have ample bark shredded from Grandmother Birch. Your fire is nearly gone, and this will give us flame very fast. To that, I will add the dry lower branches from the spruce. Easily broken into manageable lengths, they will catch the flame and pass it to the larger pieces I have brought."

The older man showed neither disappointment nor approval, again remaining stoic and unemotional.

Four Wings bunched the paper-thin birch remnants into a small bundle, then turned his attention to the smallest dry spruce branches, breaking them into short lengths. Without saying a word, he placed the birch bundle atop the hot embers and followed with layers of spruce kindling. Within moments, the birch burst into flames, engulfing the spruce kindling. As the blaze filled the center of the rock circle, Four Wings added the larger pieces of deadwood he had collected, then, maintaining the silence within the tipi, he crossed his legs and lowered himself to the ground, substantially farther back than his earlier position from the now blazing fire.

Eagle Feather Man maintained his original position until the heat caused him to rise and move farther away. Barely noticeable was a look of satisfaction on his face as he remained standing.

"You have done well with the fire. There are many before you that have not understood the fiery birch, the small kindling, and the larger fuel necessary to maintain a durable flame."

Four Wings replied, "That is no surprise to me. Let those with eyes see the mystery of the fire."

"Tell me the mystery you see."

"I will tell you what lies behind the fire mystery." Four Wings spoke softly. "The paper from the bark of the birch tree ignites quickly and flames out without lasting. It is like a man seeking the comforts of a woman with no intention of going beyond."

Eagle Feather Man lowered himself to the ground, edging closer to Four Wings's position.

Four Wings continued, "A man that seeks a wife, like the fire, needs to offer more substance to grow together with his woman. They pass beyond the sudden heat of passion to understanding a life together. The larger wood pieces represent the mature love that has grown from the first steps. That love will last as long as they maintain it."

The older man once again sat without responding for a very long time. Four Wings poked at the fire with a stick while he waited for a response.

"You have done well. What will you offer for Gentle Breeze? I have no need for horses or other belongings. I have all that I need in this world. You must bring something very valuable if you intend to make my beautiful Gentle Breeze your woman. She looks upon you with favor, and you have proven your worth; now you must bring me something extraordinary, something unheard of by the band of Lone Horn."

Four Wings sat staring into the fire, his mind whirling.

* * *

It was the cry of the eagle that clarified things.

His meeting with Eagle Feather Man had left him with deep concerns regarding his chance to earn Gentle Breeze's hand. Her father had rejected many brave men willing to take the opportunity to win his approval. None had achieved what he had, and the next step would require more than he was sure he could provide. After leaving the fire of Eagle Feather Man, Four Wings found it difficult to concentrate on anything for more than a few minutes.

This was not something he could rush into. He must think hard and long about a gift for Eagle Feather Man. He would study the problem until he was guided by the Great Spirit to understand what he must do.

The weeks passed, and winter took a firm hold, with a heavy blanket of snow making it impossible for them to journey outside the sheltered canyon. The occasional thaw and refreeze made it dangerous to navigate the trail outside the walls, and for the first time in anyone's memory they were snowbound for nearly a month and a half.

Finally, spring broke and the men were able to hunt outside the blind canyon. They reveled in eating fresh meat—wild turkey, rabbit, grouse, and the sweet taste of venison. There came a morning when Four Wings found himself on the edge of a meadow following the tracks of a cottontail in the disappearing snow cover as the sliver of moon began to set and the eastern sky glowed with a band of red. That was when the eagle swooped within inches of his head and glided effortlessly to circle above him. It was an omen, and he immediately knew what he must do.

Four Wings remembered a conversation he'd had with a Lakota brave he befriended while protecting settlers during the brief war with the whites near the Big Stone Lake in Minnesota. This Lakota brave called the area around the Six Grandfathers of the Black Hills his home. His father was a member of the Lakota Hunkpapa band of Sitting Bull, and he told amazing stories that greatly affected Four Wings. One of those stories came into clarity with the scream of the eagle, and his mind remembered.

He returned to the canyon and began making his plans. He would head for a very specific area described by his Lakota friend, and one that was identified in a similar manner by more than one brave in Lone Horn's band. Many were familiar with the area described, but none were aware of the secret the place held. Four Wings would look for something unheard of by members of the band.

He was told that to the southwest of the Six Grandfathers was a series of jagged abutments of granite standing in a line like fingers pointing toward the sky. They held a special meaning to all Lakota, and to Four Wings their secret was even more meaningful; they could provide the gift he sought to win the hand of Gentle Breeze.

He was told that the great eagles that soared among the peaks of the Grandfathers favored this specific area. It was a place so sacred that the golden eagles abandoned their need for isolation in favor of the wonderful nesting locations amongst the spires and ponderosa pines populating this area. It was here that Four Wings would collect the gift that would deliver Gentle Breeze into his care.

During his preparation for this trip, he had taken a piece of buffalo hide from the back of a beast, selecting the thickest he could find. The hide had been tanned using old methods of boiling the brain of the animal and stirring the cauldron until it was reduced to a thick liquid that was painted onto the inside of the skin, then, after allowing time for it to season, it was scraped clean. Rubbing the hair from the outside, special care was taken during the tanning process to ensure a supple yet strong piece of leather.

He cut a piece that would reach from his wrist to his elbow, of sufficient length to effectively wrap around his arm with a full overlap. On the edge of this overlap, he drilled evenly spaced holes and strung a rawhide tie to tighten what was effectively a gauntlet over his forearm.

Early in the morning, Four Wings began the journey that would allow him to take the hand of the woman he loved. He had already won favor with his performance during the fire ritual, and he knew his gift would have to be something truly special. If the stories he heard were true, Eagle Feather Man would accept the gift he hoped to give him.

* * *

Four Wings left camp at dawn, moving with ease through the densely forested hills. Their grandness impressed him, for it was nothing like the area in which he had grown up in Minnesota. Soon the dense forest gave way to the high meadow. It was situated on the edge of a drop-off in such a manner to offer a vista that stretched for miles.

There they were; rising as monoliths in the distance. They rose above the surrounding pines like giant needles stabbing at the clouds. This had to be the place. The granite pinnacles stood out, as though planted in a row, dwarfing the ponderosa pines congregated around their base. Calculating the distance to the spires, he figured to reach them before darkness overtook him.

It became abundantly clear why the eagles loved this place for their nests. The terrain leading to the impressive peaks was almost impossible to navigate.

Cliffs, nearly impenetrable forest, and the up-and-down lay of the land required him to backtrack often to find a path around the obstacles he encountered. As the sun dropped behind them, he realized it would be best to camp for the night and resume the trek the following morning.

Not wishing to announce his presence, he slept without a fire, staying warm by using the blanket he carried over his shoulder, both ends fastened securely to his waist with a rawhide tie.

He had picked a spot that offered a clear view of the needle-like peaks. He knew that dawn would signal the time for the eagles to hunt. After climbing a good way up one of the pines under which he had set his camp, he had a clear view of the rugged monoliths. Within three hours after sunrise, he saw two nesting pairs, and he had an idea of where their nests were located on the granite outcroppings.

It was now mid-May, and Four Wings knew that the eaglets normally hatched in early to mid-April. His plan relied on pure luck; nevertheless, the omen offered by the eagle that had nearly touched his head was undeniable. His chance of winning was good if he was successful; out of the question if he failed. He intended to find a young juvenile not yet fully feathered.

Normally, the golden eagle would hatch one or two eggs. On rare occasions, they would hatch three. He had been told that the competition within the nest would sometimes result in one of the eaglets being ignored by the parent and sometimes even expelled from the nest by accident as the siblings maneuvered into position to claim the meals the parents would bring.

Four Wings was looking for any unfortunate youngster that fell from the nest and was able to survive the trip to the ground.

It was nearly noon before he decided on the area he would canvas at the base of the peaks. He had identified four nesting sites, and he intended to walk the area beneath them looking for his prize.

With the knowledge that his chances of success were minimal, success was made even more unlikely by the fact that there was a very short window of opportunity for having a young one expelled from its nest. Then there were the odds against a juvenile surviving the fall.

Nevertheless, he would walk the area, nearly one mile, three times a day.

The age of the eaglets should have been such that their fuzzy baby feathers were being replaced with real feathers, wing feathers should be in various stages of development, and another fifteen days or so would find them stretching their wings in preparation for flight.

On the third night of his vigil, after he made his evening round at the base of the pinnacles and he had just settled in for the night, a storm blew in from the west with winds strong enough to break flawed branches and even attack healthy trees, bringing them to the ground. The next morning, as he approached a clearing beneath one of the peaks, hidden in the tall, thick grass, he found the treasure he sought: a juvenile golden eagle.

* * *

Weeks passed, every day spent with Four Wings in constant contact with the bird. With the young eagle hobbled and staked to a makeshift perch, Four Wings constantly talked to the raptor while he fashioned a hood from the supple leather he'd brought with him. It was well known to the Lakota that covering the head of a wild raptor kept them calm, and for the most part, manageable.

With extreme patience, he fed the young bird pieces of meat from small animals that he killed. As time passed, the pieces became larger; eventually, a whole carcass was offered. The entire time, Four Wings talked, made clucking noises, whistled softly, and made every attempt to make himself recognizable to the bird. During the training, he removed the hood for short periods of time, extending the duration with each new day. He began to handle the bird while the hood was in place, continuously speaking softly to her.

For several days, he allowed the eagle to sit on the perch completely void of all restraints except the connection to her foot. It appeared that she began to recognize his voice and allowed him to touch her and stroke her body.

Eventually, he removed the hood, and to his amazement, she seemed to accept him in close proximity to her. Eventually, he lengthened the tie and removed the hobble, freeing the bird to fly between two perches set about thirty feet apart. Four Wings coaxed her to perch on his forearm for short periods. She was becoming more docile with each passing day.

He began to bring small game for her to hunt—rabbits, squirrels, and small rodents. He placed them on the ground some distance away, and she began to follow his commands to hunt them. Keeping her well fed, she learned to bring the game back to him. Four Wings fabricated a whistle from a piece of willow that he began to use in the training process.

It was on the day of the full moon after her capture when he released the bird's tether and the moment of truth had arrived. The bird was responding to the whistle, returning to her perch or landing on his forearm if offered. To make the gift meaningful, she would have to respond from a distance; no tethers, completely free, she would have to come of her own accord.

CHAPTER SIX

The Gift

Lone Horn's camp
August 1863

Anton and Tatemina saw Four Wings walking the trail along the precipice toward camp. Scouts had reported that Four Wings was returning after his long absence, and the two men were eager to see him.

"What do you have under the blanket, my friend?" Tatemina was instantly curious. Four Wings had contrived a frame that was large enough to cover his entire back from waist to the top of his head. Covered with a blanket, it begged an explanation.

"I have a gift for Eagle Feather Man that will win the hand of Gentle Breeze."

Tatemina studied the sight before answering. "I wouldn't bet my life on that. He has gotten comfortable having her around. It is my understanding that many have tried; many have failed."

The timing was exactly as Four Wings had planned; mid-morning was the perfect time to approach Eagle Feather Man. Four Wings knew from experience that mid-morning would find him with a clear, positive mindset. Earlier in the day, he tended to dismiss things out of hand. Approaching him too late in the day as often as not yielded a delay until the following morning. Mid-morning was the perfect time to catch him at his most vulnerable.

"No one has given or received a gift like this one. It will be enough."

* * *

Despite the heat, it was comfortable inside the tipi. Eagle Feather Man had the bottom rolled to provide a two-fistmele opening on the windward side. The result was a breeze that entered, circulated inside the structure, and exited the open top, carrying the heat from the interior along with it.

Four Wings was sitting opposite Eagle Feather Man. To one side stood his makeshift backpack carrying the eagle. The shroud had been removed and the huge bird was visible.

Eagle Feather Man spoke. "Of what interest is this bird to my future?"

The young man opposite showed no response, remaining silent for many minutes before raising his eyes to meet those of the elder.

"It was my dream that Eagle Feather Man would accept this gift as a token of my reverence for his daughter. As the eagle feather is a sign of bravery, how much more the meaning of an entire eagle to her father, for it represents not only my love for her but also the respect I hold for her father. I have not heard of such a gift given in the past."

The elder Lakota showed no reaction to the words.

They sat, immobile, for nearly fifteen minutes before the elder asked, "Does the eagle hunt?"

* * *

They watched as the eagle winged her way along the dense growth of pines. It appeared that she was heading for the far end of the meadow, away from where they stood. There was a light breeze from the southwest, not much, but enough to float the mane of Four Wings's horse.

Eagle Feather Man wore the whistle as an amulet hanging around his neck. "The eagle is gone."

"May I say to my future wife's father, blow the whistle and we shall see."

Eagle Feather Man put the whistle to his lips and blew three short blasts. There was no reaction from the distant bird.

"As I thought, she is away." The older man spoke with a certain sadness in his voice.

As they watched, the eagle dipped and flew out of sight behind a low rising hill. The two men exchanged looks.

"This is the first time she has not returned with the whistle." The disappointment was obvious in Four Wings's voice as he gazed in the direction the bird had flown.

Eagle Feather Man remained looking in the direction where the eagle had disappeared. Silently, Four Wings bent to untie his mount's reins from the low-growing bush. "I'm sorry I took your time." He grabbed a handful of mane and swung onto the horse's back.

"Not so fast, young one. Look what comes our way."

Four Wings pivoted to look toward the far meadow where a lone eagle flew directly toward the two men. As she grew closer, the men saw that she held something in her talons. Before Four Wings could dismount, she was on them, gliding over their heads. After making a large circle, she returned and dropped her prize on the ground in front of them before circling again.

"Raise your arm! Offer your arm for her to land upon," Four Wings barked the command, forgetting he was speaking to an elder. The older man complied, and as the magnificent eagle approached, she glided, then flared to a standstill while wrapping her talons around the gauntlet worn on the forearm of Eagle Feather Man.

Four Wings immediately placed the hood over the bird's head and saw a broad smile on the older man's face. The trial had been a success.

* * *

The feast was one that would remain in the minds of every member of Lone Horn's band for years to come. There were speeches, dancing well into the night, and food that was forever refreshed. Anton and Star Woman were held in high esteem as Dakota relatives that had been welcomed into the Lakota band of Lone Horn. Four Wings acted out his capture of the golden eagle with much aplomb, bordering on untruth, but nevertheless in the spirit of the evening and well received by the Lakota hosts. The highlight of the celebration came when Many Feathers, son of Eagle Feather Man, danced with thanksgiving for his life, delivered by Four Wings during the rescue on the prior year's buffalo hunt.

The evening ended with a beaming Four Wings watching Eagle Feather Man lead the beautiful Gentle Breeze to the center of the gathering, where her hand was placed in his as his heart soared with a happiness beyond any he had ever felt before. With their eyes firmly fixed, he drew her hand to his face and softly declared his love before pressing it to his lips.

CHAPTER SEVEN

The Contest

Four Wings watched with interest as the game increased in intensity. What began as a friendly competition moved inexorably toward a confrontation between the two remaining opponents that bordered on total domination of one over the other. The contest, initiated as a test of team cunning, agility, and durability, took on the look of survival of the fittest.

To Four Wings's left sat Lone Horn and Spotted Elk; to his right were Anton and Tatemina.

They were a day's ride from the Lone Horn hunting camp at the invitation of Oglala chief Waglula—Worm. Waglula's wife was Lone Horn's sister, and Spotted Elk was a nephew. Lone Horn had brought the three Dakota men to introduce them to his sister's son, a warrior he felt was destined to become a great war chief for the Lakota nation. He was one of the two men still on the field.

Lone Horn said, "I have watched the young man grow. When he first began to take part in raiding parties targeting Crow villages, he showed courage, making many coups. He was also a fearless hunter; he is known to have walked into grazing herds on foot and kill a beast with a perfectly placed arrow. More than once he has run on foot with a stampede with a single bull as his target."

Anton and Tatemina exchanged looks as Lone Horn continued. "He is now twenty-one years old. At birth, he was named Cha-O-Ha—Among the Trees. As his skills grew, his father took on the name Waglula, and out of respect gave his son his name, Tashunka Witko, which means His Horse Is Crazy. All Lakota bands know him as Crazy Horse."

Spotted Elk turned to Four Wings. "It is a team effort. Once a man is touched by the ball he is out of the game. When an entire team is defeated, the remaining team is the winner. It is not often that the game comes down to a match between two men. This is the first time Crazy Horse has participated in the game. His opponent, Quaking Aspen, has been on the winning team the past three years."

The two were remnants of their teams, six players each side, and they chased a ball made of bone with their lacrosse wickets with the ferocity of a war battle. The field was nearly a half-mile long and a quarter-mile wide. As players were eliminated, the field area got smaller.

Quaking Aspen had the ball. He made a wide circle while Crazy Horse danced in the center of the open area.

The five men watched as the two closed, Crazy Horse engulfed in his dance while Quaking Aspen waited for the perfect time to strike. With a mere sixty feet between them, he acted, arm flashing downward as the trailing wicket propelled the ball toward the dancing warrior.

Without missing a step, Crazy Horse pivoted and knocked it to the ground with the handle of his wicket. To everyone's amazement, he simply scooped it off the ground and flicked it into the air, allowing Quaking Aspen to recover it without advancing from his position.

Showing no emotion, Quaking Aspen snatched the ball and took a step forward, cocked his wrists, and released the ball to catch Crazy Horse as he rebounded. The distance was a scant forty feet. With the release, he knew the toss was perfect; contact and victory was a moment away.

As the ball rocketed toward him, Crazy Horse focused on the surface of the spinning orb. He bowed his torso to the right and moved his wicket into position inches from his left hip.

The ball rattled off the hoop and glanced into the net portion of the wicket.

Quaking Aspen looked on in disbelief; the swift action by the warrior he faced bordered on the supernatural. As Four Wings watched in amazement, Crazy Horse charged toward the stationary Quaking Aspen while holding the wicket in his right hand, extended forward rather than raised in preparation for a throw.

Quaking Aspen recovered his senses and dove at the charging warrior in a desperate attempt to bring him to the ground and recover the ball. With careless ease, Crazy Horse somersaulted over the diving body while extending his wicket and allowing the ball to contact the warrior passing below him.

The game was over.

* * *

Separate groups congregated in a makeshift manner around the massive fire that roared in the middle of the assembly. The talk throughout the groups centered on the performance by the young Oglala brave.

"I do not remember a triumph as that which we saw here today," Lone Horn said. He was addressing Waglula, husband of Rattling Blanket Woman and father of Crazy Horse. "My nephew is a fine warrior; I look forward to introducing my Dakota friends to him. Four Wings, who you have met, looks forward to speaking with your son."

"As my son is impressed with Four Wings's capture of the eagle. The story is known throughout the camps. He is looking forward to meeting your guests."

The evening was filled with celebration, and the two young men found much to talk about. It was early morning when Crazy Horse and Four Wings left the rest of the party and walked to a separate campsite on the outskirts of Waglula's summer camp. What had begun as a conversation around the capture of the eagle had evolved into a burgeoning friendship between the two.

Four Wings had heard stories about the reclusive nature of the man he now sat with, but he found him to be interesting and more than a solitary person by choice. It may have been Four Wings's description of his early years along the Minnesota River that interested Crazy Horse and encouraged his trust, but they began sharing stories of hardships and triumphs, laced with the natural joys of being alive. They spoke of hunts, weather events, and war with neighboring tribes. It occurred to Four Wings that Crazy Horse was lonely for conversation with a peer, a conversation about life with no aggrandizement or superficial veneer in an attempt to impress.

They truly liked each other. This shared respect allowed them to talk about things that were normally internalized. Four Wings told of white men he respected and Crazy Horse told of those he hated. With drastically different experiences during their youth, each shared their personal views, and each considered the other's point of view.

The conversation turned darker when the subject broached the white traffic through the Black Hills and the thoughtless advance of white men with little regard for the land or its indigenous occupants. Four Wings had experienced many of the same things, and he understood the concern voiced by Crazy Horse. With the discovery of gold in the Oregon Territory, the trail to the goldfields brought the prospectors south of the main hunting grounds on the established Oregon Trail.

"They are like locust; they spread and devour all they touch. It is not healthy to have them crossing our land. Is this how the war in Minnesota began? Didn't the people fight to keep their land?"

"There were many white men that shared their good fortune with the Dakota people. The early settlers were as brothers." He was cut short as Crazy Horse erupted.

"If they lived as brothers, what was the war about? Who started the fighting?"

Four Wings, startled by the abruptness of the question and the anger in his voice, paused to consider his answer.

"When four young warriors were hunting—these were young men, never had they been in a war party—they killed five settlers, and that is what started the war in Minnesota."

"Why did they kill the settlers?"

"They killed them because of a dare between them."

Crazy Horse thought for a moment before responding. "Why was there a dare? Why were they hunting near a settlement? The deer are not found in such a place."

"That is true, but they were hunting small game, and they had firearms. They were starving because the game was scarce."

Crazy Horse absently poked a stick into the ground and pried the earth loose before he responded in an angry voice. "There are many questions about your answer, and they may be questions that cannot be answered. I would question the absence of big game; I would question the reason for the shortage of food. I would also question why you do not blame the white man for this war."

Four Wings did not respond. Crazy Horse had picked the scab from a wound that had remained below the surface, but one that was suddenly exposed, and his mind struggled to embrace the reality. *What he says is true! The war was thrust upon us.*

This manner of thinking had never entered his consciousness. It was clear that the Dakota braves had killed the settlers without provocation. *Or was that not true? They were hungry. Why was there no game?* Surely those settlers that died did not chase the game away. *But just as surely, the game was gone because of the white man.* Four Wings's mind was unsettled.

D. A. Swanson

CHAPTER EIGHT

The Last Hunt

Lone Horn's Camp

Since their return from the contest at the Oglala camp two months earlier, Tatemina had been experiencing bouts of coughing accompanied by a high fever. It had been an unusual fall with mild weather, and his sickness was disturbing. His coughing bouts sometimes lasted for many minutes. Unsure of how to care for their friend, or what was causing the illness, Star Woman and Anton took turns attending him for days on end. They had moved him to a temporary shelter near a stream where there was access to fresh water with which they cooled his torso to combat the burning fever. It was also used to saturate cloths to place upon his forehead.

Gradually, he seemed to improve. Everyone breathed a sigh of relief when, on the fifteenth day, he decided to move back into his own tipi, and life returned to normal.

A short time later, Anton and Star Woman were relaxing in their shelter. "Tatemina told me he would like to have deer meat to eat this winter. He wants to go on a hunt before the cold weather arrives."

Star Woman just looked at her husband. "Are you telling me that he intends to go on a hunt so soon after he seemed to have one foot in the grave? Husband, are you as crazy as he is? You tell him no. You tell him how we worried when he was so sick. I will go with you on a hunt, and we will get him his venison. Do not let him talk about a hunt this year."

* * *

"Are you sure you can do this?" Anton had used all his persuasive powers to convince his friend that a hunt would be a bad idea.

"Nonsense, my friend. I feel better than I have for many months. It will do me good to go on this hunt."

"By damn, you are the most stubborn man I ever knew. I'm gonna catch it from Star Woman. She's the one that's worried sick about your health."

"Tell Star Woman I am as healthy as ever. I will not take chances."

Anton relayed the message to her, she recoiled, and they both accepted the fact that he would not be dissuaded.

"Please keep an eye on him; he's been through a tough couple of weeks, and I'd feel a lot better if he would take it easy for another week or so."

Anton said, "I'll do my best, but he's old enough to know what he wants. I can tell you have never tried to change his mind after he has decided to do something."

"Just the same, keep a close eye on him."

Anton nodded. "I'll do my best."

* * *

Anton and Tatemina were eight hours northwest of Lone Horn's winter camp. As requested by Tatemina, they were on their hunt to bring deer meat to the entire band. The two had brought an extra horse to help pack out the meat they intended to get. They followed the ridge tops to avoid encountering the increasing number of whites heading for the goldfields in eastern Oregon that were now in the newly established borders for Montna Territory. The white men were becoming a nuisance but were allowed to pass through the land as long as they did not set camp.

"We've seen a dozen men with pack animals heavy with supplies. I figure it's just a matter of time until they decide to stop in the hills and settle," Tatemina worried.

"Judging by the way things rolled out along the Minnesota River bottoms, I think you might have just seen the future. The treaty of '51 guaranteed the hills to the Sioux, but we have seen how much those treaties mean when the government decides they want a better deal."

"I'll say this, Lone Horn and all his people will fight to keep this land. Our future is in keeping the whites moving and not allowing them to settle in."

Anton did not answer as he reined in and slid off the mare's back. Standing with his shoulder against her withers, he lifted her left foreleg, probed her hoof, and extracted what was causing her to limp slightly.

"Did she pick up a stone?"

"Take a look at what she picked up." Anton motioned to Tatemina.

Tatemina extended his hand, and Anton dropped the object into his palm. Bringing it into full view, he stared at what he held, comprehension making him shiver as a chill shot through his body. "Is this what I think it is?"

Anton swung onto the mare's back. "Sure as hell looks like gold to me. That there chunk could spell the end for our people here. Imagine all them that's going to the goldfields west of here." He guided the mare to stand beside Tatemina's stallion. "Have you heard anyone back in camp talk about gold in the hills?"

"In all the times I joined the elders to share wisdom, only one man, Flying Crow Speaker, ever spoke of gold. Another promptly shut him down, and it never was discussed again. I figured it was his failing health; he tends to drift off whatever is being discussed. He is a very old man."

"This here is more reason to keep the whites from settling anywhere near here. What happened in the Minnesota Territory—broken treaties over the land—has the potential of being much worse in these hills if the white man knows there's gold here."

Tatemina flipped the irregular gold nugget, and Anton snatched it from the air. "You best keep it under wraps where nobody can ever see that thing. What you hold in your hand could draw the white man like a gut pile draws flies."

* * *

The two rode on in silence; the terrain was changing. The high ridge tops were evaporating as they transformed into low, rolling hills. Between the hills were shallow valleys intersected by streams originating in the high ground. Many of the valleys, where the soil was thick from centuries of run-off from the higher elevations, produced grasslands and dense stands of burr oaks interspersed with cedar swamps that held water throughout the summer months. It was a place that held numerous whitetail deer. It was the place they would call home until they had gathered enough venison to be shared with the band of Lone Horn.

They had entered the area that had been described to them by Eagle Feather Man as the spot that held many deer over the winter months. He was sure that since the snow would return any day, it would already be a favorite spot for rutting males to look for does that would congregate there.

They had lost sunlight, and dusk was already turning to dark. It was the time of the new moon, and the darkness was total.

Anton and Tatemina set a makeshift shelter along a south-facing boulder line overlooking a vast willow swamp. They spent the night and rose early the next morning. Their sleep habits had them awake well before sunrise, the new moon assuring an inky blackness.

Tatemina was the first to speak. "Last night was a mild one. I closed my eyes and didn't know a thing until they popped open this morning."

"I'd like to say the same, but with all your grunts and snorts, I'm lucky if I slept more'n an hour or two." Anton delivered it in an affable manner not uncommon between the two of them.

"Might be a good idea to carry something you can stuff in your ears when things start to go bad for you."

The two shared a laugh and then turned serious.

Anton was chafing at the bit to get started. "We know there's a lot of sign and heavy trails in and out of the swamp. What do you think if I head to the far side, giving a wide berth and doing my best to stay downwind? You can scout this side and pick yourself a good spot to set up and wait while I mosey through the middle of that swamp. Should be able to move something your way."

"I figure we need four or five deer to feed the camp. If you get a shot, make sure you take it."

Anton answered, "If I can sneak within range, I'll take it with my bow. No sense in spooking everything our first morning."

"I'll do the same. If things work out, we should have fresh venison for dinner tonight."

The two men parted, Anton heading to the swamp's far side, Tatemina intent on finding the most heavily beaten trail exiting the swamp.

Two hours later, Anton had located a fresh, heavy trail leading into her depths. There was a light drizzle, and he felt a niggling of cold on the back of his neck, very different from the autumn weather that had been predominant until now.

His rifle was back at camp, and he carried his bow and four arrows in his left hand and a single arrow in his right as he crept forward. As his mother had taught him, he avoided walking directly on the trail, instead staying to one side. He heard her voice: "Walk little—look much."

She had made him sit in a single spot for an entire day watching the behavior of the nature that surrounded him. He had watched a red fox hunting for a meal and witnessed its soaring leap straight into the air before falling in a perfect arc to drop on an unsuspecting rodent. He had watched a hawk dissect and eat its unlucky prey as he sat motionless fifteen feet away.

Most impressive, he had seen a whitetail deer take nearly an entire afternoon to traverse a mere one-hundred yard area; a single step, nibble on green shoots, pause in mid-step to listen and smell the environment before placing that foot on the ground and advancing six inches, all the while searching with her ears, nose, and eyes for anything that didn't belong. At one point, he was close enough to see her impossibly long eyelashes. His mother had taught him well, lessons that were still ingrained even though they were learned fifty years in the past.

* * *

Tatemina loved hunting when there was a sprinkle of light rain for the quietness it brought to the woods. Damp leaves didn't rustle when walked upon, and the moist ground silenced a careless step landing on a hidden twig. Since this occasion would find him patiently waiting for the animal to come to him, he had completely different feelings toward the light rain. It was uncomfortable, and after a short while he began to feel a chill entering his body.

It was cool but comfortable when he and Anton left camp before dawn, and he expected a mild day, perfect for being in the woods. However, after setting himself up in a location adjacent to the trail he had chosen, there was a definite nip in the air, and the temperature had dropped. With the passing of another hour, he began to shiver as the temperature continued to plunge.

Another half hour and the drizzle turned to light snow while the wind kicked up, driving the swirling flakes into the crevasses and plastering the windward side of small trees and bushes with a wintery mix.

Within ten minutes, the light snow turned to a heavy blanket as the winds increased and the snow penetrated everything that was exposed; swamp grass became a wavy sea of white rolling in the distance, deadfalls turned to white horizontal walls as the heavy snow drifted on the leeward sides, filling the voids beneath. Visibility dropped to a mere ten feet.

Tatemina knew he could be in trouble when his bow slipped from his grasp and he was unable to make his fingers pick it up.

Fighting the wind and driving snow, and unsure whether the direction he traveled was bringing him closer or farther away from the safety of the camp, for the first time in his life he began to feel helpless. The pelting snow hurt his eyes, but he was able to snap a cedar branch, dense with needles, and hold it above his face to block the wind and keep the stinging pellets from reaching his face as he moved.

* * *

On the other side of the swamp, Anton knew the signs of what was to follow. Raised until his mid-teens in the mountains of New Hampshire, he had seen similar storms develop in like manner. His mother had taught him the signs, which somehow never occurred on the relatively flat prairie land in Minnesota. With a sure knowledge of what was to come, he immediately began to retrace his steps and return to camp, breaking into an easy jog when the terrain permitted. He arrived when the weather transitioned to a full-scale blizzard.

Tatemina was not there.

* * *

Anton felt the heat radiating from the fire now blazing near the boulder wall they had chosen for their campsite.

It had taken him longer than he liked to gather kindling and the necessary dry wood to construct the fire, but it was now well established, and he could feed it with larger logs tapped free of excessive snow. In addition, while becoming increasingly anxious about Tatemina, he hastily fortified the makeshift shelter with thickly needled branches broken from the many red cedars close to the camp. It was now time to search for his friend.

Reassuring himself that the horses were out of the fierce wind and their hobbles were intact, he struck out in the direction he knew Tatemina had taken.

The occasional break in the wind offered a momentary visual reprieve, allowing him to see trees that appeared as mere shadows at a distance of nearly twenty feet. To ensure that he could retrace his steps, he snapped branches as he moved, knowing their protruding stumps would act as trail markers to find his way back to camp. More than once he made the mistake of confusing a low-growing cedar with the outline of his friend, only to be disappointed as he drew closer.

All at once, they stood face-to-face as Anton circumvented an immense oak tree. Anton was shocked at the condition of his friend. His face was nearly as white as the snow, and his body was hunched, arms hanging loosely as he fell against Anton's chest.

"Tatemina, are you all right?" Immediately, it was clear that he was not all right. "Can you walk a little farther? I have a blazing fire at camp, and it's not far from here."

He was met with a blank stare that made his breath catch in his throat.

Embracing his friend and helping him stay upright, the two of them fought the wind and headed to the life-saving fire one hundred yards distant.

The boulder near which they had made camp was on the leeward side of the wind and nearly devoid of snow. Helping Tatemina sit to one side with his back to the boulder, Anton worked at nudging the fire away from the rock wall to uncover the warm earth where it had burned for the past few hours.

Anton was kept busy gathering wood, feeding the fire, and maintaining a vigil over his friend. Around midnight Tatemina, who was sleeping, began to grow restless, moving his legs as though trying to keep his balance, an arm moving in spasmodic jerks. A while later he began speaking gibberish. With deep concern, Anton determined that he had a raging fever, perspiration soaking his clothing.

Doing his best to keep cool moisture on Tatemina's forehead, Anton cut off a corner of his blanket and filled it with snow, carefully holding it close to the fire until it melted, saturating the fabric, which he used to wipe his friend's forehead.

By dawn, the storm had moved through and the sky cleared. Anton wasted no time in locating two poles with which to make a travois. Tatemina was in no shape to ride back to Lone Horn's camp, and he knew another night here might prove to be too much for either of them.

With the travois attached to Anton's horse and Tatemina's stallion tied in line with the pack horse, they set out for Lone Horn's winter encampment.

* * *

"I knew it was too soon for him to do this. Anton, you should not have taken him on that hunting trip. He was far too weak."

"Star Woman, hear me, there was no stopping him from doing it. I'll bet he would have gone alone if I had refused to go with him."

It was two days since Anton had reached the camp, and during that period Tatemina had never been alone. Gentle Breeze and Star Woman had taken turns being with the very sick man, giving him water and broth and watching over him, doing their best to make him comfortable.

"Yes, I'm sorry. It's just that he is very sick. It seems he can hardly breathe at times, and I am worried about that cough."

Just then, the flap parted, and a breathless Four Wings entered the tipi. It was clear that he had run some distance.

"Gentle Breeze wants you to come now. It is Tatemina; he has taken a turn for the worse."

The three of them burst through the flap and ran as fast as they could toward the shelter where Tatemina was being tended. He was close to a fresh-water source in a tipi normally used for holding rations while the band was on the trail of the buffalo.

Four Wings was the first to reach the tipi. Knowing what awaited them, he stood to one side and allowed Star Woman to enter, followed by Anton.

"Oh no." Star Woman's response was heartfelt and filled with pain. "Oh no. What in the world happened?"

Gentle Breeze responded in a near whisper, "He started talking without making sense. The words were as foreign words; I could not understand him." Eagle Feather Man, who stood behind the others, had joined them in the tipi.

Gentle Breeze continued. "He spoke in a quiet voice until he went into a fit of coughing. It went on and on; I thought it would never end. The coughing made him short of breath. He breathed in gasps between coughs. Blood began to form at the corners of his mouth. He laid on his back while the horrible coughing continued until the blood began to flow down the sides of his face, as you see him now."

The others looked upon the still body of their friend. There was absolute silence that seemed to carry on forever. After several minutes, Star Woman spoke. She spoke from her heart, words that reflected her learning during translation sessions of the Bible from French into the Dakota language when they were in Minnesota Territory.

"Tatemina, you are a brave and honorable man. You saved many lives in the battles of '62 and nearly died on the gallows with the thirty-eight. You have now gone to the grandfathers. They will treat you well, for you have lived your life with thoughts of others. We will miss your presence, your wisdom, and your strength."

Opening her arms, she turned to indicate the canyon outside the tipi. "This spot will be perfect for our noble friend. The earth will never freeze, and the grass never stops growing. It is here that his body will rest until he is called home to join his soul and spirit now in the presence of the Lord."

He was buried in the hidden canyon where the band of Lone Horn spent winters. Across the stream from the location where his life ended was a sheltered nook. The space was positioned as though it had been carefully placed to catch the winter sun where the soil never froze, and the small creek continued to run all through the winter months.

CHAPTER NINE

Red Cloud

June 1865

S ince their meeting at the contest, Crazy Horse had ridden west to the Tongue River to see for himself the trails now being broken by the white prospectors on their way to the Montana goldfields. He had followed the Tongue River to its intersection with the Yellowstone River. Once there, he rode east, crossing the Powder River on his way back to the Black Hills.

Crazy Horse was now in the camp of Lone Horn, visiting with Four Wings. "It is good to see you again, my friend." Four Wings had welcomed Crazy Horse, who was seated opposite Gentle Breeze in their shelter. Truly excited by the unexpected visit, Four Wings offered him a bowl of the stew simmering on the small fire and reached out for the hand of Gentle Breeze as Crazy Horse wiped his bowl clean with a sizable piece of fresh bread.

"I have come from the Powder River Country, where I have met with Arapaho and Cheyenne warriors. The buffalo range is healthy. There is a new trail reported to be the main route to Bannack and the gold find reported there."

Gentle Breeze interjected, "The route being followed is along what they call the Oregon Trail, well south of our main hunting ground."

Crazy Horse stared at her, sternness written on his face. "What you do not know, you should not speak of," he said with an air of dismissal.

He continued, focusing his reply toward Four Wings. "A new trail has been established by a man named Bozeman. It follows earlier trails but has been forged through land that will support wagon movement." He paused. "It also runs through the middle of our buffalo hunting grounds."

Gentle Breeze curtly excused herself and stood facing Four Wings, her back toward their guest. "I will go now to visit Star Woman."

Four Wings was silent until she left the tipi.

"My woman is protective of me. She means no disrespect."

There was no comment in return.

He continued, "What of this new trail? What can be done?"

"I came here to ask if you would like to ride with me to see what may be done to close this trail. I will understand if you choose not to go with me."

"Now why would that enter your mind? Because of what my woman has said? Do not worry; I make my own decisions."

* * *

Having been told of the new trail established nearly a year earlier to function as a direct route to the western Montana goldfields, the Bozeman Trail was being used in direct disregard of the 1851 Fort Laramie Treaty. Crazy Horse wanted a council with the Oglala Sioux named Maȟpíya Lúta, who refused to stand aside and allow the incursion into traditional buffalo land. He wanted to speak with this Oglala the whites called Red Cloud.

The temporary camp was well situated on a hill seventy yards from the only cattail swamp within thirty miles. The swamp area had developed in the shallow swale as a result of prior years of flooding. An early growth forest populated the high ground with a few cottonwood trees near the swamp, giving way to pines as the elevation increased. There was no way to approach the area without crossing miles of open prairie.

Crazy Horse and Four Wings approached the camp with great caution. They had been told that the man they sought would be found here, but with the influx of white prospectors using the newly established Bozeman Trail,

Crazy Horse never let his guard down, always aware and always ready to fight or run, whichever the situation dictated, and Crazy Horse hated to run.

It was early evening, and the setting sun promised a repeat of the sunlight and parching temperature that had accompanied the riders the past two days. In spite of the heat, they couldn't ignore the beauty of the evening—a blazing red sky intersected at intervals by cumulous clouds reflecting that sunlight to the distant mountains composing the Bighorn range.

Dismounting at the camp's edge, Crazy Horse raised his arm. "We wish to speak with Maȟpíya Lúta. I am Tȟašúŋke Witkó, known to the whites as Crazy Horse."

"And I am Red Cloud. I know of your presence in our country here. I have known for two days. Come sit with me, and we will talk."

Three warriors appeared from nowhere, one taking the reins from the two riders, the other two moving to flank Red Cloud.

"We have come to learn of your plans to deal with the white incursion into our hunting grounds. With me is my good friend, Four Wings."

Four Wings spoke. "I know of Red Cloud. Your strength is well known among the Miniconjou band of Lone Horn."

"I have heard of both of you. One, for your abilities to fight," He nodded in the direction of Crazy Horse. "The other, for your eagle gift to the Miniconjou Eagle Feather Man." His eyes looked Four Wings up and down before settling on his face. "All my people know of this gift."

The statement both embarrassed and filled Four Wings with pride. He had no idea that his gift was known by the great chief Red Cloud.

The men settled in to smoke a pipe and engage in what could only be described as small talk, during which they began to feel comfortable with one another.

After considerable time was spent in this manner, Red Cloud changed the direction of the conversation. He said to Crazy Horse, "I have heard of what happened to our Dakota brothers and sisters when the white men moved into their land." He turned his attention to Four Wings. "I would like to know how the battle began along the Minnesota River. The white men are now coming into our land, land guaranteed to us in the Treaty of 1851. I think we must fight to keep them out."

Four Wings, having been exposed to Crazy Horse's views on the evil brought by the whites, answered, in what he thought was a well-balanced statement.

"There is a difference between what happened there and what is happening here. We lived in peace with white traders before the army came. We had many white friends. But it seemed the army wanted our land for their own. They have broken many treaties and cannot be trusted."

Red Cloud listened.

Crazy Horse took up the argument. "They now pour through the land of our Six Grandfathers and have made a trail through the heart of our country on their way to dig the Montana gold. This is not right."

Red Cloud poked at the fire embers before responding.

"As I say, we have seen what has happened to our Dakota brothers. It is not an easy thing to say we will fight the whites, just as it is not an easy thing to ignore their trespass on our land. I have thought many days about this problem, and I think it is best if these gold seekers turn away of their own accord."

"They will never turn away without blood being shed; we must attack these rows of wagons and make them turn away," Crazy Horse spoke from his heart. "Nothing we can say will stop them, only fear of dying."

"Yes, Crazy Horse is right in saying that only fear will stop them, but there are ways of creating fear other than by surrounding them with death. I do not believe the answer is in starting a war with the whites. Such a thing was tried in '62, and where did it lead? It led to the destruction of families and total defeat. I do not want that for my people."

The three men talked until all had been said on the topic, Four Wings speaking only when asked about what had happened in Minnesota, each maintaining his position on stopping the encroachment by the whites. They parted friends but with very different philosophies on protecting their land, their homes, and their mainstay, the bison. While Four Wings had great respect for his friend Crazy Horse, he understood Red Cloud's hesitancy to attack in an all-out war on civilian wagon trains. Both men had a point, but he felt himself slanting in the direction of the militant Crazy Horse.

* * *

Crazy Horse and Four Wings were now approaching the western edge of the Black Hills. The entire distance from their meeting with Red Cloud, there had been few words spoken between them, each man sifting what had been said and looking to resolve the conflict those words had caused in their minds.

At one point, Crazy Horse posed a question. "Do you think there is honor in allowing the white prospectors to cross our prime buffalo land?"

They rode for several minutes before Four Wings responded. "I think there is little honor in killing women and children being brought upon our land by white men seeking gold." They rode on for several more minutes before he added, "I think killing all the whites will draw many soldiers to our land. More than we can defeat."

The two rode on in silence for a long time as Crazy Horse pondered his reply, finally saying, "I would have no hesitation to kill them all and send a clear message to the Great Father in Washington that the Lakota will protect what is ours. Do not think for a moment that allowing the wagons to cross our land will prevent a war with the whites. Have you not seen enough to know it will result in more and more abuse of our people? More and more incursions into our land?" Crazy Horse was becoming angry. "I have thought much about this."

From that point onward, there was no conversation as each man searched inward, each weighing what the other had said, both aware that each of their views was subject to reproach.

CHAPTER TEN

Stop the Incursions

July 1866

Ever since the Oglala contest won by Crazy Horse, Four Wings had found himself examining his life's purpose. It was the question posed by his friend—*Why do you not blame the white man for this war?*—that played on his mind.

Oglala Chief Red Cloud hosted the 1865 tribal games, though the excitement proved subordinate to anger at the white invasion. Several bands had sent representatives to the games because their chiefs were unable to attend. Such was the case with Lone Horn's band. He, along with Anton and Spotted Elk, were dealing with trespassers entering the Black Hills, so Lone Horn had chosen Four Wings to accompany Many Feathers, the son of Eagle Feather Man, to represent his band. Four Wings was pleased to see Crazy Horse representing a band of Oglala warriors.

Following the games, tribal chiefs met to discuss what was happening across the frontier and to explore efforts to deal with the encroachment. Appeals to the US government had proved ineffective, and many were advocating for the destruction of the wagon trains crossing Indian land.

"As the gold plays out in one area, it is discovered in another," Red Cloud said. "Miners are crossing our land to reach new goldfields. Mostly, they travel west along the Oregon Trail, which follows the North Platte River for much of the way. They go through our land, but most go south of prime ground. But new goldfields have been discovered in Montana Territory."

It was unusual for Red Cloud to engage in a conversation such as this. Those present knew the importance of what was being said.

"They have established a new trail that shortens the distance to reach the goldfields. It crosses Powder River country, cutting through our prime buffalo range to reach Virginia City." This entire area had been guaranteed Indian land in the 1851 Horse Creek Treaty, and white incursion was prohibited.

"I know most of you want to kill any white man that comes upon Indian land." He surveyed the gathering of chiefs as heads nodded and raised fists filled the assembly.

"I will fight the army and any man that tries to steal our land." He paused as others murmured their agreement.

"But to war with all the whites by attacking the wagons and killing women and children would bring the might of their army to drive us off the land. We know what happened in '62 when our Dakota brothers rose up against the whites in like manner. Have we not learned from their mistakes?

"We know that the Horse Creek Treaty guarantees this land to be ours. Now the army is building a fort on the Powder River in violation of the treaty. I will control the whites entering the new trail they call the Bozeman. My fight is with the army and prospectors that violate the treaty. I would take responsibility for the Powder River country."

Four Wings, seated with Many Feathers, listened to the proceedings. He turned to his young friend. "Do you see the wisdom in what he says?"

There was no response from Many Feathers.

An argument ensued, primarily fed by the outrage of the younger warriors. "We will kill all whites that enter our land," said one.

"I am not afraid of the army. Let them come with all their guns. We will defeat them," said another.

The older warriors that had seen much war were quiet as the tension rose among the gathering. Finally, Red Cloud spoke again.

"Hear me!" Respect for the man viewed as a main Oglala chief stopped the braggadocio coming from the younger men. Red Cloud was not a chief because of his bloodline, but instead because of his wisdom and performance in battle.

"This is not a decision to be taken lightly; we must agree, and we must honor that agreement. I claim responsibility for stopping the building of forts on the new trail. I will do it while fighting the army, and I will try to avoid killing women or children. I will halt the advance of prospectors and settlers across our land."

Order was restored, and individual tribes talked, and responsibility was claimed for protecting homelands or hunting grounds. There was universal agreement that if at all possible, no innocents would die. Red Cloud gained the support of the Northern Cheyenne and Arapaho warriors, both of which would benefit by stopping movement on the trail.

On behalf of Lone Horn, Four Wings and Many Feathers claimed responsibility for leading the effort to keep the central Black Hills free from white settlement.

* * *

It was mid-afternoon a month or so later when Anton, Four Wings, and Spotted Elk moved toward a spiral of smoke with extreme caution. Most of the whites that were asked to reroute, after being told the promises to the Sioux as stipulated in the Horse Creek Treaty, known to them as the Fort Laramie Treaty, were willing to modify their route or travel through the hills without stopping.

Anton had been in this area before during one of his many successful attempts to dissuade white travelers from using the Black Hills as a primary route to the goldfields of Montana. Three days ago, a Dakota brave had ridden into the buffalo camp of Lone Horn to warn the people of a seven-wagon train two days east of the hills, moving west.

As prearranged, Anton, mounted on the bay mare, walked her toward the makeshift camp with no attempt at concealment. He rode on the trail cut by the wagons as they rolled through a broad expanse of open land running in a natural valley. Unseen, but moving adjacent to him, the others mirrored his approach.

The wagons were spread in a line, oxen unhitched and grazing on the ample grasses. Men, women, and children were busy doing chores in preparation for setting camp for the night; the young were searching the area for dry wood at the edge of the tree line while the women did the necessary things to set camp. Some staked canvas tent structures from the wagon beds, others prepared beds adjacent to the wagons, and others planned to bed down under the wagons themselves. The men were tending the livestock and checking the condition of traces and harness leather and ensuring that wheels were greased and in generally good repair to resume the journey in the morning.

Anton had walked the mare past four of the wagons without attracting attention. When he reached the fifth, he saw a young boy running ahead, he assumed to inform the next wagon that a man was riding through the train. By the time Anton passed the sixth wagon, he was the center of attention.

As he approached the lead wagon, he saw men distributing themselves in defensive positions and closing the path he'd used to advance to his present spot.

He reined the mare in and sat calmly astride her bare back.

"Hello, train master, my name is Anton McAllister. I have come to greet you as a friend." He spoke loudly, to no one in particular. "I have come to meet the leader of this train and talk about measures to ensure safe passage to the Montana goldfields. Please hear me as a friend: I have information for the wagon master that will protect your train and see you safely through the Sioux land you now camp upon."

A voice bellowed from behind the wagon.

"Come ahead so I can get a look at you."

Nudging the mare forward, Anton rounded the wagon. Drawing on the reins, he stopped dead in his tracks. There, to his right, was the largest man he had ever seen. He was huge; each of his massive hands was easily the size of both of Anton's placed side by side; above his barrel chest were shoulders that looked to be three feet wide, and placed squarely in the middle was a perfectly round head completely devoid of hair. And the most bizarre thing: the man was sitting in a rocking chair, and across his lap lay a shotgun.

"You want to talk to the wagon master? Well, here he is. Climb down off that horse and let's hear what you got to say."

Anton slid off the mare's back, "Am I right in thinking you're on your way to Montana gold?"

The man stood, stretching to his full height, and the top of Anton's head came no higher than his chin. "Might I ask why that would be any of your business?"

Anton replied, "You know you're on Sioux land here in these hills?"

"Says who?"

"Says the Fort Laramie Treaty. It's been that way since '51."

"I guess I'd have to call that tough shit, mister. You supposed to be some authority or somethin', or are you jest a troublemaker?"

"I'm not looking for trouble, just trying to tell you how it is; this here land belongs to the Lakota Sioux, and they don't take it lightly when a train of wagons comes rolling through." Anton could feel the animosity building. "Look, mister, you got women and children with you, which is why you ain't been bothered yet. I figure it would be to your advantage if you just keep moving."

"Them women and children you talk about are the reason we aim to set camp and spend the night right here. We figure we can also round up some venison for a good hot meal. Ain't no Injun gonna miss a couple of deer."

Five of the men with the train were ambling in the direction of the lead wagon, leaving two others unaccounted for. Anton hoped that Spotted Elk and Four Wings had incapacitated both.

The big man moved closer to Anton. "You lose your saddle, or do you like riding like the damn Indians? I think it best if you jest slide back on that horse and get the hell outta here before somethin' real bad happens."

"Let's not let things get carried away here. I come with a friendly warning and advise you to either continue until you clear the hills or turn around and skirt them to the south." Anton turned slightly to position himself broadside in front of the wagon master. "Do yourself a favor and back off."

The big man took a step forward. "I warned you, mister, now I'm gonna show you what real-bad feels like."

As the man's lead foot hit the ground, Anton grabbed the horse's mane and raised his leg, propelling it sideways as hard as he could, jamming it into the big man's kneecap. He heard a popping sound as the joint separated, and the big man went down, pain distorting his face.

Grabbing the shotgun from the ground where it had fallen, Anton raised it and slammed the side of the barrel into the man's forehead, knocking him unconscious. Then he lifted the muzzle in the direction of the others. "Anybody else think it's a good idea to camp here?" The men looked from one to the other as Four Wings and Spotted Elk appeared from behind the adjacent wagon, urging the two missing men forward to join the others.

"You men pick up this giant fool and set your families to loading them wagons. You can move forward or back the way you came, but know one thing: you will not spend the night in these hills. If you got a way to spread the word east, let them know anyone coming into the Black Hills will run into a passel of men that intend to keep it free of white settlement."

CHAPTER ELEVEN

The Fetterman Fight

I n 1865, to protect white prospectors and settlers moving west on the Bozeman Trail, the Federal Government launched the Powder River Expedition and appointed a commission to study the problem in direct disregard of the 1851 Fort Laramie Treaty, which promised the country to the Indians and banned the white men from entering.

In late August 1865, Brigadier General Patrick E. Connor began to build Fort Connor on the Powder River to protect travelers on the Bozeman Trail. In November of that year, the fort was renamed Fort Reno in honor of Major General Jesse Lee Reno, who died in the Civil War battle of South Mountain in Maryland.

Major General John Pope, commander of the Department of the Missouri, had ordered Colonel Henry Carrington to staff Fort Reno and to build two additional forts farther north. Carrington, an engineer and a graduate of Yale University, was a former professor of natural science and Greek at the Irving Institute. During the Civil War, he organized Ohio regiments and was involved with non-combat assignments.

He began construction of Fort Phil Kearney in July of 1866. Located on a natural plateau between Big and Little Piney Creeks just north of the Powder River, the fort would be the largest constructed along the Bozeman Trail.

Red Cloud viewed the fort's construction as treachery. The white men had asked for permission to use a road, but before hearing the answer they had already brought soldiers to build forts along that route.

Crazy Horse was in Lone Horn's winter camp speaking to Four Wings. He was seeking support for Red Cloud in stopping the construction altogether. The two men were on open ground some distance removed from Four Wings's tipi. "I think you understand why we are not in my shelter."

"I have an idea why that is, and I am glad for it. Your woman is very protective and speaks boldly of her views. Lone Horn has four warriors that wish to fight with Red Cloud to protect the buffalo ground. We will ride west in the morning and gather others as we ride. I hoped you would go with us."

Four Wings replied, "It is the season of the snow. There is little hunting, and we have much wood for our fires to warm us. I will talk to Gentle Breeze, and I will join you."

"Your woman will not like it."

"Gentle Breeze knows that many died in the early Minnesota war with the whites. She will not like it, but she will not stand in the way. What is happening here is not the same as it was there. Here, the fight is for a specific trail on land granted to the Indian."

* * *

The construction of the fort had been under constant pressure from the Indians. The wood trains—oxen-pulled wagons—being dispatched the five or six miles to reach the pine trees in the Bighorn Mountains to collect wood for the build had been confronted by Red Cloud and his men from the beginning. With the realization that travel in the bottomlands always resulted in attacks, the army began to send the wagons out along the ridgelines and open areas where it was more challenging to stage a surprise attack.

Carrington placed spotters on the high ground, Sullivant Hills, where they could monitor the trains' progress and signal the fort when the harassment began, at which time Carrington sent out a relief party to chase them away.

Construction continued throughout the summer and into the winter. Every step of the way Lakota warriors, along with Arapaho and Northern

Cheyennes, gathered with Red Cloud to harass the wood-cutting parties and slow down construction of the fort.

Carrington realized that Red Cloud was using these incidents to draw the soldiers into ambush situations. His response was to order his men to keep the skirmishers at bay and not pursue them.

The majority of officers under Carrington's command had led Civil War battles and were proud of their fighting abilities. In fact, after defeating General Robert E. Lee and the Confederates during the war, they were almost universally of the opinion that the poorly armed Indians were little to fear. It was the opinion of the majority that Carrington was passive to the extent of being cowardly. In actuality, he recognized the situation as it was and knew the limitations of his small command and the strength of the Indians.

* * *

"If you ask me, I say we take it to these red bastards and drive them clear out of the territory—or kill them all. To me, it makes no difference." The speaker was Lieutenant George Washington Grummond, a cavalry officer. Several officers had been sharing stories of their Civil War escapades when the conversation turned to the current predicament they faced. "When we get delivery of them new rifles we oughta ditch these muzzleloaders and make short work of it. Them boys won't know what hit 'em." A few of his men carried Spencer repeating carbines, and their firepower was immense compared to the standard-issued muskets.

"I, for one, came to this damn frontier to eradicate the red menace that stops our progress. It's time we took an active role in eliminating them," said William Fetterman, a November arrival at Carrington's command who was convinced that the passive resistance offered by the army had led to the situation they now faced. Fetterman had proven his fighting ability during the Civil War and had been made a brevet lieutenant colonel. He was of the opinion that Carrington was a timid commander bordering on incompetent. With great respect for the position but little respect for the man, Fetterman was a constant thorn in Carrington's side.

"I do not doubt that a single company of regulars would have little trouble in whipping a thousand of these warriors. It is time we break this virtual standoff and give them the hell they deserve."

The fort's quartermaster, Captain Fredrick Brown, added his voice to the conversation. "You boys know I'm chomping at the bit to put an end to this damn business. Seems the fort's near done and Carrington is showing a mite more mettle with protecting them wood trains what's getting us our lumber." He paused to take a sip from the bottle being passed between the three men. "I want to be the one that takes Red Cloud down; in fact, I want it so bad I delayed my transfer out of here. I'm itching to fight and hoping to get a chance at killing the bastard."

Captain Fetterman broke in, "I'm thinking along those same lines; in fact, I figure if I had eighty good men, I could ride through the entire Sioux Nation."

* * *

Four Wings sat at Red Cloud's fire inside his shelter. To his left was Cheyenne Chief Dull Knife, to his right Crazy Horse and High Back Bone, a Miniconjou who had been with Red Cloud for some time.

Red Cloud felt strongly that bringing death to all who entered Indian land and killing the white families without provocation would only enrage the government and guarantee retribution upon his people. However, as hard as Red Cloud tried to avoid direct attacks on wagon trains carrying women and children, he eagerly brought the fight to the US Army and settlers that failed to heed warnings, and he fought them every chance he got.

"We have seen much success in stopping the wood-cutting parties and delaying the build of this fort they call Kearney," High Back Bone said.

Dull Knife replied, "We slow the building, but we are not stopping them. They place men on the high ground to signal the fort when we attack the wagons. Troopers are then sent to drive us away."

Four Wings's appreciation of Red Cloud's methods was growing with every meeting with the great chief, who now addressed both him and Crazy Horse. "My Lakota brothers are great warriors. I will welcome Crazy Horse to stop the army from building forts along this trail."

Crazy Horse responded, "I see much wisdom in Red Cloud's methods. There is honor in killing white soldiers. Your method of attacking the wood-cutting wagons on their way to the Bighorns has slowed their building of the fort. Do you not think it is time to do more, to give the white invaders reason to leave this place?"

Red Cloud's eyes took on an intense glare as he responded, "There is little chance of us attacking the fort. It is strong, and we are in the open as we approach. I will not place my men in such danger."

"Red Cloud is right," Crazy Horse said. "The soldiers must be outside the fort, as they are when they protect the woodcutters. They will not have cannons, only what they can carry on horseback. I would like to offer a way to strike a greater blow than the current raids upon the wood-cutting trains. We must send a message that they will understand."

Red Cloud nodded in agreement. "Do you have a plan?"

Crazy Horse thought for a time before answering.

"We use baited traps to catch wild animals; in the past, I have baited a trap to catch white men. With the right bait, we can lead them into a death trap. They lose all reason if they see a chance to kill a warrior—how much better if they see the opportunity to kill several?"

* * *

On December 21, 1866, Red Cloud had his men positioned to attack the wood train as they had done before. Unless there was a drastic change in army policy, he knew that the protection detail would chase the attacking party away from the train.

On this morning, the lookout on Sullivant Hills signaled that the wood train was under attack about a mile and a half from the fort.

Carrington had prepared his relief detail as he had done in the past, ordering Captain Powell to drive the Indians away and not pursue them into an ambush situation.

Fetterman, citing his brevet commission from Civil War days, demanded leadership of the relief party, and based on his brevet rank, he was given command of eighty men. Forty-nine infantrymen on foot, Lieutenant Grummond and twenty-seven cavalrymen, Captain Brown, and two civilians with Henry repeating rifles.

"Now we can show what well-trained troops can do, eh, Captain?" The question was directed at Captain Brown, the man that had delayed his transfer in hopes of killing Red Cloud himself.

"Yes, sir, I'll finally get a crack at taking Red Cloud down."

* * *

Four Wings, for the first time in his life, was committed to supporting his Lakota brothers in a fight against the US Army. He had been placed in a position to observe army movements when they left the fort in support of the wood-cutting detail, and he was to relay information to Crazy Horse if they deviated from routine.

The Miniconjou warrior High Back Bone appeared to the support party from a safe distance. He and six of his men were feigning injury in an attempt to draw troopers in their direction. Afoot, they were easy prey begging to be killed. However, the relief party unexpectedly veered to charge toward the far side of a butte called Lodge Trail Ridge. From that direction, they would flank where the wagons were being attacked and circle behind the Indians.

Four Wings raced along a hillside trail and quickly reported the move, allowing Red Cloud time to reposition his warriors in anticipation of the battle about to unfold. From his new position, Four Wings, with a clear view of the opposite side of Lodge Trail Ridge, bent, hands on knees, to recover his breath after his mad run.

The plan had called for Crazy Horse to act as bait, dismounted and leading an apparently lame horse over the crest. Four Wings watched as Crazy Horse appeared at the ridge leading his horse. Once clear of the ridgeline, he mounted and rode the narrow trail, weaving between boulders and breaks in the rough terrain to a shallow swale where he swung to the ground, looped a rawhide tie around the horse's front fetlock, and pulled her hoof off the ground. Four Wings looked on in amazement as his friend offered himself on open ground.

Four Wings involuntarily sucked in a breath when he saw the army appear on the ridge. It looked like they were breaking pursuit, but only for a moment;

the army commander raised his sabre and charged onto the trail, attention focused on the Indian with the lame horse.

The entire command had cleared the ridge and were moving toward the open ground when all hell broke loose.

As Four Wings watched, the entire hillside came alive. Warriors filled the open area behind the charging riders, making it impossible for them to retreat, and it seemed that every boulder, every break in the terrain, and every growth of sage turned into screaming death. Over two thousand warriors—Sioux, Arapaho, and Cheyenne—filled the air with arrows while troopers tried in vain to reload their single-shot muskets as arrows, lances, and tomahawks brought death without pause.

When the fighting ended, tens of thousands of arrows had been shot, and the entire command was destroyed. Fetterman and his eighty men were dead, their bodies mutilated; body parts severed, eyes gouged, skulls bashed in, and brains scooped out and placed upon rocks. Entrails were placed on adjoining rocks.

Four Wings watched from a distance as the warriors desecrated the bodies of the slain. Brave men, likely men with families, were being hacked to pieces. He knew death and was not afraid, but he was not prepared for the sheer barbarism taking place in front of him. He turned away, shaken to his core.

Red Cloud had delivered a message: we will protect this land.

* * *

The celebration lasted for two days, during which the victors danced and reenacted brave deeds done during the fighting. On the eve of the second day, when many warriors had retreated to their shelters, Crazy Horse and Four Wings had retired to a tipi removed from the others. The excitement of the battle was now a memory, and the two of them spoke in guarded terms; Crazy Horse because he sensed disapproval from his friend, and Four Wings because he feared the ugliness of what he had witnessed.

"Our brothers fought bravely. I think the army will question the use of this trail."

Four Wings thought before answering. "The defeat could not have been more clear. Do you believe the Great Father in Washington understands the meaning?"

"I believe what happened will put fear in the hearts of those wishing to take this trail to the goldfields. I believe we have proven our ability to protect our hunting grounds. It is the Great Father in Washington that will see what was done here and think hard about the cost of using this trail. There are other trails they can use; others that do not threaten our prime buffalo grounds."

The two men sat in silence for several minutes before Crazy Horse spoke again.

"I sense that you disapprove of what was done here. Is this how you feel?'

"Crazy Horse must understand; the defeat of the army in this fight was a good thing. Your warriors earned a great victory," Four Wings paused, "and the army learned a great lesson."

Crazy Horse opened his mouth to reply, but Four Wings raised his hand to silence him.

"I felt pride in the victory, but I felt shame when the dead were cut to pieces and made as waste. You are a great warrior and a brother, but I cannot be a part of such needless things as what was done after the battle. My brother, I will fight with you, I will protect your back. The Lakota are great warriors, and I am proud to be your brother. The crazed eyes I saw as men hacked away at men already dead went beyond what I think of as honorable. Will you understand my desire to be with my family in the hills while I consider what has happened in this place?"

Crazy Horse sat immobile, eyes fixed on a distant thought. He remained sitting cross-legged near the fire that burned between them, his thumbnail absently scratching at the bark on the stick he used to prod the fire. After a very long time, he spoke.

"I favor our friendship. I respect the ways of the Dakota, and I understand your early life with the whites. Clearly, your ways are different from mine, but I will respect them as you respect my ways. Four Wings is a good friend, a true brother, and will remain that as long as I live. Go back to your family."

CHAPTER TWELVE

Crazy

Black Hills, 1867

Arnold Quarterman was no longer seeking his fortune. He now thought of himself as the justified executioner of all who trespassed on this land. Rarely spending more than a single night in the same camp, he roamed the land without a destination, his only goal to eliminate tresspassers.

There was another equally bereft of logic; only this man was a Dakota Sioux who had lost his mind while living as an outcast from his brothers, banned because of his extreme cruelty. His name was Crazy Otter and he, like Arnold Quarterman, roamed the prairie and rugged landscape.

Completely alone, he fought his war against the whites, and every white he happened upon fell to his cruelty. He began stalking individuals, skirting settlements looking for the single man that he would capture and, at a location distant from civilization, torture to death. He was like a ghost, making sure he interacted with no one. There were the occasional small groups of Indians, also anxious to avoid detection, and those he avoided as though they carried the plague. He trusted no one. He had only a single thought in his mind—kill the white man.

It was late fall when a cold snap forced him to curtail his self-appointed job as executioner and find a place to spend the winter. Coming upon a small lake in a depression nearly a mile wide, he swept the perimeter for signs of life. Seeing nothing that indicated human visitors, he discovered a game trail that had fresh sign leading from a stand of cottonwoods skirting a small swamp. Strewn across the entire perimeter were deadfalls, branches, large cottonwood trunks, and smaller swamp willows.

After going over the entire area and seeing nothing he would view as a threat, he began to consider it a place to winter. The swamp was nothing more than a pocket, stretching about three hundred yards across and twice that distance from end to end, but the vegetation was so dense he felt it fruitless to try to explore the area. It seemed the only thing missing was a source of fresh water.

Undecided about making the area his winter camp, he backtracked to the small lake. Searching the surface with his eyes, he noticed a dark spot on the snow-covered ice just off the shoreline. Stepping onto the ice, he approached the place for a closer look. Without warning, the ice gave way under his feet, and he found himself nearly chest-deep in clear water. He broke through the thin ice between him and the shoreline, and he realized he had discovered a spring that fed the lake. Here was his water source.

After warming himself by a hastily constructed fire, he built a rather substantial shelter between two standing cottonwoods. Skinning the bark from the most massive downed tree and placing it over a frame made with dead willows, he formed a structure that resembled a combination of a wigwam and a lean-to. The overlapping bark would divert rain and snow, and the layers proved to be excellent insulation from the cold. It was all but invisible from a distance yet gave protection and heat retention almost as well as any other structure he knew.

He settled in. His killing would have to wait.

The morning after the third night in his new camp, he struck out for the lake to fill his water bag. Cresting the rise above the swamp, he froze in place; not thirty yards in front of him was a wolf feasting on what remained of a deer carcass.

"Heyeah—get out—heyeah—heyeah!"

Hanging from the beast's jaws and blood-covered snout was a long piece of sinew.

Not expecting anything such a short distance from his camp, Crazy Otter had only his knife. When the wolf showed no fear, the reason for the Indian's name became evident. Yelling at the top of his lungs and waving the water bag in one hand and the knife in the other, he charged the animal.

The wolf stood facing him as Crazy Otter closed the distance between them. When only fifteen feet remained, the wolf became unnerved, turned, and bounded away. Crazy Otter, yelling at the animal, mainly out of fear, circled the dead deer. The kill was so recent the wolf had only begun to feast. He had torn open the underbelly of the animal and eaten the organs; it had just started on the rear haunch.

This is good. He viewed what had just happened as a sign. *There is nothing to stop me from killing the whites. Wolves fear me; I shall bring death to the whites.* Had he been a wolf himself, his hackles would have been on end as every fiber of his being came alive. With thoughts only of killing his enemies, he began to circle the carcass in a wild dance, singing a song with no words, as though being led by Satan himself. Every so often he stopped the chant to offer a promise. *I will kill all I come across, be they Indian or white; if they are dressed as a white, they will die.*

He danced, chanted, threatened, and then danced some more. Clearly, a dark force that was to lead him to greatness had entered him. He would never die in battle—he knew that for certain.

The winter was mild by plains standards, and his shelter was placed at the perfect angle to catch the warming rays of the midday sun. In fact, it was so comfortable that he had trouble abandoning his small camp, staying there until early May.

The small lake had been clear of ice for three weeks, and the greening of spring was changing the landscape. There seemed to be a frantic impatience within the animals. Waterfowl came and went, the songbirds trilled their morning songs, and the rodents darted across the well-packed floor of his shelter. The fire inside him again blazed as the weather turned, and his intense hatred of the white man drove him on his quest for vengeance. Crazy Otter broke camp and resumed his campaign against the whites.

He was now atop a butte far west of the Missouri River.

* * *

Arnold Quarterman rode along the bottom of the Butte singing at the top of his lungs:

"O, I wish I was in the land of cotton,

Old times there are not forgotten,

Look away, look away, look away, Dixie Land.

In Dixie Land where I was born in,

Early on one frosty mornin',

Look away, look away, look away, Dixie Land."

As he had done for the last twenty minutes, at the completion of the chorus he pulled his pistol from his belt and fired at the first thing he saw. If one were to retrace his route, one would find bullet scars on rocks, bullet holes in the occasional tree, and a plethora of holes scattered around bushes and in shadows on the ground.

Crazy Otter watched in fascination from the top of the butte as Arnold moved through the area below. While most Indians avoided contact with a person considered to possess a demon, Crazy Otter viewed it as a gift. How much fun would it be to kill this white man? The fact that he was minute in stature only enhanced his anticipation for the act. He had no idea that the man he was about to kill was motivated by the same emotion, just aimed directly at him.

Arnold had seen the man on the butte as he approached the incline long before the man on top sensed his presence. Aware of the native fear that insanity could be contagious, he played to his audience of one. The high ground stretched for about another quarter mile before sloping down to the level on which he rode.

With no embarrassment whatsoever, Arnold swung his arms to the music, often shooting his pistol into the air to punctuate song verses, then reloading as he rode. Approaching the end of the raised land, his guess for where the ambush would take place was foremost in his mind as he scanned the ground ahead. Unless he had misread his assailant, he expected a face-to-face standoff.

There had been many places that offered the perfect opportunity to kill him with a rifle if that was the man's only intent. Arnold's years as a bounty hunter served him well in reading other men. This one would want to take him head-on, allowing for delivery of a slow and painful death.

He couldn't help but smile as he imagined the look on this Indian's face when he realized he was about to die.

Seeing the logical ambush spot, Arnold completed the final chorus of "Dixie" with a flourish, drew his pistol, and emptied it into the air. As he slid the empty revolver into his waistband, the Indian walked his horse to block the trail.

Arnold acted as though he was addressing a friend as he switched songs with a flourish and began the chorus of the second song he knew, "Rose of Alabama."

"Oh brown Rosie,

Rose of Alabamy!

A sweet tobacco posey

Is my Rose of Alabamy."

A broad smile crossed the face of Crazy Otter. Now he would have some fun. He had never before had the opportunity to torture a man possessed such as this. He knew the man had emptied his pistol, and there was little to fear as the two approached each other. Casually sliding his hand across his midsection and letting it settle on the hilt of the knife sheathed at his waist, he caressed it before slowly slipping it from the sheath.

While the Indian was preoccupied with the knife at his waist, Arnold started the next verse as the horses met and stopped walking:

"I landed on the far sand bank . . ."

He began to sweep his arms in a grandiose manner.

"I sat upon the hollow plank . . ."

His left arm swept outward from his waist.

"And there I made the banjo twank . . ."

His left arm rose above his head, and his right began to raise, palm down.

"For Rose of Alabamy."

At the last word, his right arm stopped moving upward, and Crazy Otter saw the Derringer pistol and knew he was dead. It was the last thought he had as Arnold Quarterman pulled the trigger and the bullet slammed into the bridge of the Indian's nose, directly between the eyes, bowling him backward and spilling him to the ground.

Arnold began to giggle. The giggle became a maniacal laugh as wave after wave of uncontrolled laughter poured from his mouth. Suddenly, he stopped laughing and jumped to the ground.

From behind his back, he produced a tomahawk. He began hacking away at the body until he stood holding Crazy Otter's scalp along with a good portion of his skull. He walked to his horse and placed the scalp in a blood-encrusted bag tied behind the saddle. He turned and walked his horse to stand beside the corpse, upon which he stepped to gain access to the stirrup, and climbed aboard.

Without a sound, he urged the horse forward.

"O, I'm glad I'm not in the land of cotton

Old times there were soon forgotten . . ."

CHAPTER THIRTEEN

The White Man

In April 1868, Red Cloud went to Fort Laramie to discuss a new treaty. Far-reaching in its scope, the new document made modifications to the 1851 treaty signed at the same location seventeen years earlier. This treaty met Red Cloud's demands but contained enough technical jargon to confuse even the white officials.

The government didn't stop at closing the Bozeman Trail. The Fort Laramie Treaty of 1868 clearly defined the Great Sioux Reservation, which included the Black Hills, and further guaranteed the "absolute and undisturbed use and occupation" of the entire land reserved for the Lakota people. It contained a clause designating the land north of the North Platte River from the western limit of the Black Hills, and west to the Bighorn Mountains as Unceded Indian Territory, with the provision that no whites would be permitted to settle in the Unceded Indian Territory without Indian permission. Lakota lands were to be inviolate, the peace permanent.

"We have done well with our battles," Red Cloud said to his warriors. "I urge the young warriors to abide by this agreement. It says we will not fight; it says they will deal with whites that come onto our land if we report it to the agent. I have their word."

With his mark made on the treaty papers on November 4, 1868, Red Cloud had won his war.

Relative peace covered the Black Hills in '69 and '70, while farther west and to the south conflict was steady as the native tribes fought among themselves and against the whites to maintain control of what they considered their land.

* * *

Lone Horn's band continued to prosper, and good fortune followed them on their annual buffalo hunts. More and more, Gentle Breeze and Four Wings lived outside the group moving with the vast herds, more to satisfy their need to be alone together than the actual hunt, for when they stayed in the main camp, Eagle Feather Man maintained a constant presence. Ironically, his fear of losing his daughter caused him to spend as much time as possible in her company, which worked to force her farther away. When he began to join them every day, they decided to move from the hills entirely.

On the fifth of July 1873, they bid good-bye to their families and struck out for points north. Four Wings and Gentle Breeze knew they must begin their lives anew, and that meant they must start those lives on their own. With no surety of where they would finally settle, they left Lone Horn's camp amid bittersweet blessings from friends and family.

Gentle Breeze had received assurance from Star Woman that she and Anton would watch over Eagle Feather Man. "Do not worry unnecessarily about your father," she had said. "Anton will keep him busy watching over the security of the hills. It will do your father good to be involved in maintaining the hills for the Lakota."

As they rode from the camp, Gentle Breeze realized what they searched for would be difficult to find without traveling all the way to the mountains of the new state of Montana. But she knew where they would set camp on their first night, and her heart stirred with excitement at the prospects of what lay ahead.

They rode little-used trails through the most beautiful part of the hills. Their goal was to make camp at a small lake that Gentle Breeze had visited with her father when she was ten years old. It was the most beautiful place she had ever seen, and she had never forgotten it. It was the one place she wanted to revisit before leaving the beautiful Black Hills.

The first hour of travel found both of them lost in their separate thoughts. Finally, Four Wings broke the silence.

"I fear the future for the Lakota, especially those in these hills. I am not worried about our families—our fathers can persuade the traveler to go elsewhere—but the first whites allowed to enter and stay in the hills will start a flood, and, as happened everywhere to the east, our people will be displaced."

"Do they not know that we won't be intimidated?" Gentle Breeze asked. "Red Cloud has managed to keep them from the Powder River country. It seems they are not beyond reason."

Four Wings was skeptical. "We will see."

As they wove their way through open meadows, around heavily treed abutments, and along high ridge trails strewn with boulders, the immenseness of their presence in the middle of a vast prairie was spellbinding.

"We are almost to the stream that empties into the lake."

They had been riding for hours, and Four Wings was thoroughly confused. Confident that they were moving north, they would come to an area that offered open sky only to reveal they were actually moving east. His childhood in the relatively flat landscape of Minnesota had done nothing to prepare him for this land.

Riding up the slope from the broad meadow they had just crossed, Gentle Breeze pointed to a rock face barely visible through a cleft in the trees.

"That is where we will find our place to set camp. You will see it is the most beautiful spot in the world. I would like to rest there and enjoy the sweet smells I remember as a little girl; they are impossible for me to describe, but they are wonderful." She nudged her horse to allow her to touch Four Wings on the thigh. "I am excited to share this with you. You will see such beauty."

She led them on without comment, and he followed. Finally, as they rounded a wall of granite, they looked upon a hidden jewel nestled at the base of ponderosa pines that reflected their beauty in the clear, blue-mirrored surface.

"It is breathtaking." Four Wings was mesmerized. It was as though they had entered a different world.

The water from a mountain stream settled into a depression to form a small lake covering about forty acres. The layout was such that the shape of the lake resembled that of a nesting crane, the nest represented by the cattail swamp along the northern edge where the water grew stagnant, and wildlife found it extremely accommodating.

They dismounted and walked to sit on the trunk of a fallen tree.

The smell of the wet, loamy soil deposited over the years brought to mind his childhood and the hot summers spent with his mother along the Minnesota River. She had taught him to appreciate the rejuvenating aroma of the swamps after a summer rain. Drawing closer, the sound of the frogs and crickets swept over him like a wave as they sang the melody of the forest.

"Isn't it wonderful?" Gentle Breeze closed her eyes and tilted her head toward the sky. "Isn't this the most beautiful place on earth?"

"It is amazing."

"It is good to be alone with you, my husband."

"As it is with you, Gentle Breeze, so it is with me. I love every moment we have together."

"This is like no other place in the world. It hasn't changed a bit since my father first brought me here. It is good to know that the treaty guarantees it will remain Sioux land forever, I don't think I could bear it if it was lost to the white man."

He twisted his body to gaze directly into her eyes and took both of her hands into his.

"I have seen the white man take the land from east to west. Their appetite for land is never satisfied. The Northwest Territory was wild and free, and they sent an honest man to watch over it. That man was Lawrence Taliaferro, and he governed with regard to the Indian."

He raised her hand and touched the back of it to his lips before holding it against his cheek. "This business of white men marching through Lakota land is the same as what happened in Minnesota. Crazy Horse has made me see things that I did not see before." He moved her hand to his other cheek. "I fear for the people."

She placed her free hand to the back of his head and drew him to her chest. "Red Cloud has shown strength. We are strong. Best of all, we have kept the hills for our people."

They sat that way for a long time, wholly immersed in each other's company.

As dusk settled in, they talked about their good fortune at finding one another. Four Wings recounted the meeting of Spotted Elk and acceptance into Lone Horn's band of Miniconjou Sioux, which led to their meeting. She remembered Four Wings's courtship and his gift of the eagle to her father.

Before they knew it, dusk had turned to darkness.

"The grass is plentiful and will make a wonderful base for our bed. If you set a picket line for the animals, I will gather grasses." Four Wings rose to his feet.

The two of them were as gleeful as children on an adventure spurred by the moment. Four Wings, using his knife as a sickle, cut and gathered bundles of the soft, pliable grass to spread as bedding under their blanket while Gentle Breeze tended to the horses. The August evening was warm, bordering on steamy, and they planned to leave at first light to clear the hills and start the trek westward in earnest.

They sat together enjoying the symphony of the forest in the darkness, and the sky came alive with uncountable points of light as they displayed the universe in all its glory.

Gentle Breeze broke the silence. "Do you think our people will ever be forced to leave the hills?"

He turned his head to stare at the calm surface of the lake. After several minutes, he spoke.

"What happened to the Dakota ten years ago—"

A ruckus erupted within the trees ten yards from where they sat. Instinctively, Four Wings dove to his left, catching Gentle Breeze in the crook of his arm and pulling her with him as he somersaulted into the darkness. The moment they settled, he released her, rolled to his feet, and without pause sprinted to circle behind the commotion as a wild turkey emerged from the now dark stand of pines and low-growing bushes, wings beating loudly.

As the massive bird crashed through the branches, Four Wings eyed the area, looking for whatever had startled it from its roost. With quiet returning to the forest, he carefully prowled the perimeter of their camp, knife in hand, searching the shadows, smelling the air for the odor of mountain lion or bear, and listening for unnatural sounds in the night.

After a thorough check of the area, he returned to the camp, where Gentle Breeze waited.

"Well, that was exciting." She spoke with a certain amount of relief in her tone.

"I'm not sure what happened, but it startled the hell out of me. Let's get some sleep. We may be able to figure out what scared it come daylight."

With that, the two curled together on the grass matt that was their bed.

"Four Wings . . ." she whispered.

"Do not be troubled. We are safe."

"I know." There was a long pause. "Do you think our people will be able to stay in these hills for the remainder of their lives?"

"I hope that will be the case, but things seem to be repeating. There is an unmistakable likeness to what happened in Minnesota before the hangings."

"Oh, I pray that it will not be repeated here."

"So do I. The new treaty allows us to stay on this land. We should be safe here for a long while. I am concerned about those that have chosen to continue hunting and living in the unceded land to the west. They have chosen to continue living as in the past, while those living on the reservations will receive guaranteed benefits under government protection."

* * *

Gentle Breeze was the first to awaken. The day was well underway with the sun nearly popping over the hill to the east. Four Wings lay with his back to her, peacefully unaware of the lateness of the day. She decided to let him sleep.

Carefully, she rolled from the blanket and looked over the small lake. There was a translucent mist floating above the glassy surface of the water, tendrils waving upward to disappear into the sky. As she watched, an imperceptible breath of air caused the mist to shift to and fro in a silent dance.

On the shore, thirty or so yards distant, was a mother deer and her spotted fawn, mouths dipping to the water as they drank. The doe lifted her head and looked in Gentle Breeze's direction, water dripping from her chin. Satisfied that there was no danger, she resumed her morning drink.

"Beautiful, isn't it?"

She was startled by his voice. Spinning around, she was engulfed in his arms as they embraced.

"Let's have a look and see if we can figure out what caused that commotion last night."

Together, they walked around the low-growing bushes to where a stand of bur oaks grew close together. Four Wings examined the areas around the base of the trees while Gentle Breeze made a broader circle some distance from the oak trees.

After a short while of searching, she heard his voice. "I've found the perch that the tom likes to use. It looks like he's been here more than once judging by the spattering of droppings underneath this tree. Have you seen anything that could have made him fly?"

"As a matter of fact," she said excitedly, "I see some scrape marks that look fresh." She squatted to get a closer look. "Come here and take a look at this; it doesn't look like an animal did this."

He kept his eyes on the forest floor as he moved to join her.

"It sure looks like a pair of boots made these scrapes, doesn't it?"

Dropping to his knees, he carefully brushed dried pine needles and last year's leaves to expose the soil. Working in a semicircle, he was able to determine the direction from which the man had either approached or exited the area. One thing was sure in his mind; an Indian did not make these tracks. A few minutes more searching the ground, and he found prints made by a shod horse.

"Four Wings, you better come over here."

Sensing tenseness in her voice, his head snapped in her direction.

She was staring at a pine taken down by the winds of last winter. "I think I see what caused the turkey to fly."

Three strides had him standing next to her. He followed her pointing finger to see a barely visible toe of a black boot protruding from under a covering of broken sticks and bunched leaves.

"You there, come on out; we will not fire." More than anything, Four Wings wished he had his rifle in hand. He had no firearm, and a bluff like that could go wrong in a moment.

There was no movement from under the tree.

Skirting to the right, he quietly approached from the opposite side.

"C'mon over," he called to Gentle Breeze. "This man likely died during the night. Help me drag him out, and we'll see what we've got."

The two of them cleared the debris from around the body, debris intended by the man to hide him before he lost consciousness.

He wore deerskin leggings of the type worn by the Sioux. They covered the tops of black boots, the kind used by the whites, but different than those worn by the army. He wore a blue waistcoat of the same appearance as those worn by the soldiers, with two rows of brass buttons down the front and epaulets on the shoulders indicating the rank of an officer. On his head was a knit cap common among the voyageurs of Four Wings's past.

While Four Wings searched the body for weapons, Gentle Breeze brushed pine needles and dirt from his face. She noticed a twitch in one of his eyelids. Moving her ear to the man's mouth, she listened for breath.

"This man is not dead!"

"He's still breathing?" Having finished his search for the man's weapons and finding nothing, he turned his attention to the man.

"You think you can help me move him?"

* * *

The man lay unconscious under the shelter of the lean-to just constructed. Gentle Breeze cleaned his wounds and wiped his lips with a cattail root soaked in a warm broth concocted of wild plants known to have healing qualities. A further search for weapons turned up only an empty knife sheath strapped to his waist just under his coat.

After washing away the dirt and grime, his injuries became evident. Under blood-soaked and matted hair, a deep gash on the right side of his head, just above the temple, had crusted over. Centered on the back of his head, well below the crown, was a swelling nearly the size of Four Wings's fist.

His body was lean, an indication of an active life. His palms were calloused and broad, fingers short and large in diameter. Both hands contained significant scarring, common among mountain men of the day, evidence of living in the wild. His hairline nearly connected with his eyebrows, and a beard, trimmed on a regular basis, was as black as midnight.

And most notable—he was a white man.

"I've never seen this man, but he looks to be familiar with the wild. I'm thinking he's been living alone, maybe a mountain man, but I haven't heard of them being here in the Black Hills; far as I know, they roam the big mountains to the west. I never figured they'd be this far east."

"What do you think happened to his weapons? Surely he had a rifle. And what happened to his knife? His sheath is empty."

"That's a darn good question. Does that wound look like a knife made it? It seems too irregular to me." Four Wings was looking closely at the gash on the man's head. "It almost looks like someone took a chop with something that had a dull edge. I've never seen anything like it before."

They had removed the man's coat and were working on his shirt. The shoulder was soaked with blood and still bleeding; Four Wings cut the sleeve away to get a clear view of his wound.

"Well, don't this tell a story. It's pretty clear what happened to him."

Gentle Breeze examined the wound while Four Wings began cutting strips of the shirt to act as a bandage. The shoulder had evidence of what started as a puncture wound that widened to a trough, exposed flesh hanging as though shredded. Lifting his arm to reveal the side of his chest, she saw another gash similar to the one on his head.

"What in the world caused this?"

"I'd be willing to bet anything that this man tangled with a mountain lion."

Four Wings reexamined the head wound and looked carefully at the shoulder and chest wounds.

"That gash on his head and the one on his chest are from the cat's claws." He shuddered involuntarily at the thought.

"That shoulder is what the hellcat grabbed with its fangs; looks to me like he almost missed. I got a feeling it was a young lion. Mature hunter wouldn't have missed the initial attack. Either that or this guy almost dodged the whole thing altogether."

Gentle Breeze poured water over the shoulder wound as Four Wings continued to examine the man.

"That tooth plowed right through the flesh. Lucky it didn't get to the bone. I'd say that's the only reason this guy is still alive. Must have been quite a fight. It looks like the cat had a hold of his shoulder and raked the side of his head and chest with its claws."

They checked the rest of the body; there was no blood anywhere else on the man's clothes.

"This guy killed that animal, or he wouldn't be here. I think that's what happened to his knife—lost it in the battle and didn't pick it up."

There was silence between the two while Gentle Breeze continued to clean and dress the wounds, the only sound that of the drumming of a ruffed grouse echoing across the lake. At the scream of a blue jay, Four Wings said, "This man is no soldier."

* * *

Four Wings and Gentle Breeze sat at the fire, comfortable with the silence between them. Each searched their private thoughts regarding this unforeseen impediment to their immediate future. Four Wings, whose past had placed him in close proximity to white settlers and fur traders, viewed this man as simply a man. A man who was injured and might not live through the night. His instincts told him he must care for this stranger. Gentle Breeze felt differently.

"I think we must stick to our plan and leave this place. We have cleaned this white man's wounds and done what we could to make him comfortable. What was he doing here in the hills? Perhaps he is leading a large party with the intent of settling near here." The more she talked, the more animated she became.

Four Wings stopped her. "This man has been badly hurt. We cannot just leave him here to die."

"You are right, of course. This is not like leaving an enemy to die after a battle. This one has not raised his hand against us. Tonight should tell the story. If he is still with us in the morning, I feel he will live. If not, he will be out of our lives."

Behind them, the man lay in a temporary lean-to shelter, open side facing the fire. They had placed him on a doubled blanket. He had shown no sign of life beyond shallow breathing.

Four Wings said, "I look forward to being with you." He reached out and picked a dead branch from the ground, wedging it into the burning logs. "I have heard there is much beauty to the west, where we are going."

She looked at her husband as he spoke; he squatted comfortably, poking at the fire, knees drawn to his chest, eyes reflecting the red of the embers. She had seen those eyes filled with tears at the death of Tatemina; the same eyes had been alive with excitement and promise at the buffalo dance after he had saved her brother during the hunt. Those eyes, drawing her in, were now filled with purpose, reflecting an inner resolve that she found inescapably captivating.

"Four Wings, wherever we go there will be beauty around us. We see the beauty from within, and this view of life allows you to see the best in all things." She moved to touch his forearm. "As I said, tomorrow our journey will be decided for us. If the man lives, we will be bound to take care of him until he recovers. If he dies, we will resume our move west."

"And if he lives, there is much to learn about this man; what happened to him, how did he come to be in the hills, why had he not been expelled like other whites?"

"The first step is to bring this man through the night. If he is leading others here to settle, we will convince him that it is not a place for him or his people."

* * *

Dawn found the campsite quiet; a small flame licked the edges of dead branches arranged as kindling to reinvigorate an almost expired fire. There was only stillness punctuated by the occasional call of a blue jay scolding something in the area he called his own.

"I have found where they fought," Four Wings said. "This is surely the spot where the attack took place."

They were roughly one-quarter mile up the slope to the north that they had taken to enter the sheltered lake area the day before. The combination of pine needles and leaves covering the soil was scraped to expose the bare ground. Disturbed earth made it easy to follow the fight as it moved from the trail to the undergrowth along its edge.

"This musta been some fight." Four Wings was ten feet from the trail. "I don't see a speck of blood, but there are broken bushes and snapped branches all over this area. I can only imagine what went on."

They continued the search and finally came across blood spatters on the downed leaves and a small stand of aspen with blood smeared along the trunks of a few, effectively marking the path taken during the struggle.

"Here's where something happened." Gentle Breeze squatted next to a congealed pool of blood that faded into a dry stream of the once-crimson liquid leaving the pool. She followed the blood trail for a short distance before coming to the inert body of a male cougar.

* * *

On the third day, the man woke up, bewildered and sore but able to tell them what happened. He had just mounted his horse at the top of a ridge when the cat jumped him. His horse likely saved his life by shying as the cat was in the air, causing it to miss the mark but connecting enough to drag him to the ground.

"I didn't have time to think, but I knew I was in trouble; the damn horse ran away with my rifle. My sidearm and holster were in my saddle bag so all's I had was my knife. It took a while to get the damn thing out of its sheath. It's surprising how things what used to be easy turn out to be damn hard when a lion's hanging on ya."

"You oughta take it easy mister," Four Wings interjected. "That's a bundle of talking for someone that's been where you've been the last couple days."

"I figure you're right. I got quite a thirst; suppose you can get me some water?"

Gentle Breeze headed for the crystal-clear creek where it entered the lake.

"Damn, it feels like a horse kicked me in the head. Hurts like hell." The swelling on the back of his head had not gone down.

"It's pretty unusual to see a white man in these hills. What brings you here?" Four Wings knew the impropriety of asking the question under the circumstances, but the man seemed willing to talk.

"President Grant himself sent me here to see the general attitude of the Sioux about selling these hills to the government. Rumors of gold got him thinking it could help with the shortage of money since the war with the South. He told me it could make the Indians rich if the government decides to buy them."

"Why'd he pick you to do the scouting? Where'd you come from? What's your name?"

Before he could answer, Gentle Breeze returned and set a kettle of clear water near the fire.

She dipped a cup into the kettle. "Prop him up so he can drink this."

Four Wings moved to the man's side. "Mister, here's your water."

There was no response.

"Mister." He pressed the man's shoulder. There was no movement. Gentle Breeze set the cup on the ground.

"He's passed out. I wonder what's going on with him."

"He complained of a headache. Maybe his brain got rattled when he got pulled from his horse. He was talking just like we are now, then all of a sudden he's asleep."

Gentle Breeze shook her head. "I'm not so sure he's going to be all right. He talked up a storm, and then he's gone? There's something not right. Seems a blessing if he just doesn't wake up."

"He told me the president in Washington sent him here to learn what he can about the possibility of the Sioux selling the hills to the government."

"Why him? What's his part in this?"

"Can't say. We were just getting started. All I found out was the government's short on money, and they heard there's gold in the hills. If it's true, I figure they're gonna find a way to take them."

"If there is gold, and this man learns of it, that could be a disaster for the people," Gentle Breeze pointed out.

"If there is gold here, and he tells everyone, things are gonna change. Right now all them that comes into the hills plan on going straight through to the goldfields in Montana. It'd be a lot easier if this man doesn't make it." He paused to gather his thoughts. "But I can't be the one responsible for him dying, or even letting him die if he has a chance to go on living, no matter what it could mean."

Gentle Breeze's demeanor changed in an instant. "My people have lived on this land for many years. We took it from the Kiowa and the Crow, and we kept it. It is holy to the Lakota. I will kill him if that is what it takes to keep him from finding anything here that the white men want for their own."

* * *

Four Wings left camp as the sun was clearing the horizon to the east. The substantial peak rising between them and the flat land beyond offered a significant obstacle, blocking the direct sunlight. It would be nearly an hour before it would clear that mountain. Until then, he would be in the shadows of early dawn.

Gentle Breeze was reluctant to let him go. "Please be careful."

"I'll be alright. My guess is his horse stopped in the meadow just over the rise. Wouldn't make much sense for it to go farther."

He jogged with a smooth gait toward the trail that would take him over the ridge. He had only his rifle and a pouch filled with fresh water hanging around his neck. He reached the spot where the cougar had attacked and picked up the clear trail left by the frightened horse as it hightailed it back the way it had come.

Reaching the crest of the ridgeline, Four Wings slowed to a walk to better pick up the track made by the frightened horse. To his chagrin, the small meadow he remembered crossing on the way in was now a mere depression in the land.

Realization of his flawed memory caused a moment of concern, and he wondered if the meadow he remembered would appear over the next hill. No longer confident in his recollection of the topography of the land, he carefully studied the track made by the horse that had slowed to a walk.

His confidence shaken, he was apprehensive as he cleared the next ridge, but he was graced with a clear view of a meadow at least a hundred yards wide, in the middle of which stood a paint gelding peacefully grazing the lush grasses, reins dangling from each side of the halter.

Four Wings approached the horse from the front, speaking softly, with great care to do nothing to spook the animal. Taking the reins in his hand, he began to lead the animal in the direction of his camp.

* * *

It wasn't until the following evening that the injured man once again regained consciousness and began to speak.

"Who are you? Where am I?" It was clear that he didn't remember their prior conversation.

"How long have I been here?" He looked at the bandages and felt the side of his head. His confusion began to clear as he took in his surroundings.

"You were attacked by a mountain lion. As you can see, you survived. The lion didn't." Four Wings spoke in a low voice. "My name is Four Wings, and this is Gentle Breeze. You are in our camp, and we found you two days ago. Seems like a gift from the Great Spirit that you are alive."

They learned that he lived in the mountains to the west and that he considered himself a friend of the Indian. He was straightforward in his verbal exchange and impressed the two of them with his honest questions and answers.

Twice during their conversation he tried to stand, only to be overcome and forced to sit down immediately.

The longer they talked about things of little interest to her, Gentle Breeze began to question the man's motives for being there.

"You say you have been in the mountains to the west. I am surprised you were allowed to stay there. Depending on where you were, there are Cheyenne, Crow, Lakota, or Arapaho waiting to expel you."

She stopped, waiting for his response.

"Yes, but they trusted me as an Indian. I count among my friends Oglala Chief Red Cloud and Cheyenne Chief Dull Knife. I have met Crazy Horse and found him to be honorable and a good man."

Not deterred, she decided it was time to address the main issue. "Why are you here?"

The man remained calm, but considerable time passed before he answered her question. "I am here because I was asked by important people to assess the situation with the Lakota and their attachment to the hills they call Páha Sapá. May I ask what band you are from?"

"I am Lakota, from One Horn's band."

"So you are Miniconjou." He looked directly into Four Wings's eyes. "And you?"

Without hesitation, Four Wings said, "I also call Lone Horn's band my own. I am Dakota, and this woman is my wife."

"My name is Ogden Dent. I have lived with your brothers and sisters for the past fifteen years. I am proud of my friendship with them. You do not need to mistrust me. I will always be a friend to the Sioux. They know me as Owatumla—Straight Tongue."

Gentle Breeze asked, "How is it that you are here?"

"I am here because President Grant asked me to come."

"Why would he want you to come here? It is hard to believe that he asked you to do this thing. How does he know you well enough to ask this of you?"

"His wife, Julia, is my sister."

Dead silence followed. It was as though the creatures of the forest had heard the statement, shutting their mouths and halting their actions. Moments turned into seconds as Four Wings and Gentle Breeze exchanged a look.

"I came west in '54. My sister was already married to him. Back then, he wasn't much, just a man." The man named Dent was absentmindedly scratching the ground between his feet with a stick. "I was only nineteen at the time, and I needed space. I found it in the mountains."

Four Wings said, "Seems a mite strange—just up and leave the family like that."

"I wasn't happy there. My father had slaves and had no intention of giving them up until he was forced into it. It caused a few arguments. I decided to strike out on my own. What better place than to move west? I ended up on the western side of the Bighorns."

The man they now knew as Dent abruptly turned to the side, spread his hands on the ground, and retched. Sweat broke out on his forehead as uncontrolled spasms turned his stomach inside out.

There was nothing they could do for him, although Gentle Breeze soaked a cloth in the cool water and placed it on the back of his neck. After several minutes, he lay back, exhausted and completely spent. Within moments, he was asleep.

"We got us a real sick man. Don't know what ails him, but I don't figure it has much to do with the damage the lion did. Judging by the knot on the back of his head, I'd say that's where the trouble lies." Four Wings spoke while stepping into the lake and splashing water on his face and shoulders.

"We'll see what tomorrow brings." Gentle Breeze was resigned.

* * *

The day in camp had seen her not so veiled attempt to delve deep into the mystery of the white man with the Lakota name. The possible future of all that she loved could hang on his reasons for being here. She found that after a relatively short time answering questions, he needed to rest, often sleeping for over an hour. As the time passed, she began softening her approach to the man she found difficult to dislike.

By the time Four Wings entered the camp with a large turkey over his shoulder, she was confident that Dent posed no threat to her, her family, or to the Black Hills.

"Husband, today I will make a feast for us. While our guest slept, I hunted for berries and nuts to add to our supplies. I will now use them to add to our meal."

* * *

The fire crackled and popped as the turkey rested on the spit a foot or so above the coals. With every addition of wood to keep the fire hot, Gentle Breeze turned the spit to ensure the bird was evenly cooked. It had been over the flame for the past two hours and was yet another hour away from being ready to eat.

Four Wings glanced in the direction of the shelter. "It seems you have made a decision regarding our guest."

"I believe he is a friend, but he is not well. It may take a while before he regains his health, so it is best if we remain here until he gets better."

"Then so it shall be."

It took seven weeks for the man to recover to the point that he could ride and do the things he did before he was hurt. During his healing, the dizzy spells slowly reduced in quantity and duration, but there were still bouts with unsteadiness from time to time.

The men enjoyed each other's company, often talking late into the night. He showed interest in her family and how the two of them became man and wife. His curiosity and interest in their past led to conversations normally reserved for longtime friends. They learned much about his life in the east. A strong friendship was developing between the two men, and even Gentle Breeze had found common ground with Ogden Dent. When the decision was made to move on, Dent opted to go with them to the west.

CHAPTER FOURTEEN

The Injury

1873

Lone Horn listened as a messenger from another summer encampment reported the presence of a Crow hunting party within the Black Hills. "They have already taken several buffalo from a small herd moving through the Bent Creek area. We have heard that Lone Horn is protector of the central hills."

"How many are in their party?" Lone Horn asked.

The messenger gazed at nothing in particular as he sought to remember what he had witnessed. "There are seven braves. They have pack animals, so it appears they intend to hunt until the weather drives them west with their pack animals loaded with buffalo treasure."

Lone Horn took a long time before he answered. "It is good that we keep them out of the hills. I will talk to my headmen, and we will take care of the problem."

Within an hour after the messenger left the camp, Lone Horn had gathered prominent members of his band, including Anton, Eagle Feather Man, and

Spotted Elk, and they sat in council. He opened the meeting with questions directed to his son, Spotted Elk.

"You have led the effort to keep the whites from coming into our hills. It seems as though there are fewer and fewer wagons crossing our land. Is that true?"

"Anton and Eagle Feather Man have done well at turning the wagons away from the hills. Since Red Cloud had the Bozeman shut down and the gold has played out in Montana, it is easier to control the whites that enter the hills." He gestured to the two men sitting opposite him. "They have been very convincing to those wagons not wanting to turn back, and they have done it without killing."

Having voiced his satisfaction on that matter, Lone Horn addressed his latest concern regarding the small group of Crow warriors hunting in the hills.

"We need to attend to another matter; there is a party of Crow hunters taking buffalo from our land. Although they have not killed any of our people, they have threatened that any Lakota that tries to stop them will die."

He stood, stepped to the entrance to the tipi, and pulled the flap down, sealing the doorway. Turning to face the others once more, he said, "We need to chase them from our land. Tomorrow I will take Spotted Elk with me to the agency at the Cheyenne River to speak with the agent and tell him about the problems with keeping others off Sioux land. The papers we signed in '68 guarantees this land is ours, and he must know that we will fight to keep it as ours."

"The new white chief in Washington named Grant is known as one that wants peace with the Indian Nations," Anton said. "This is what many told us when they turned their wagons to skirt the hills."

"I have heard reports that say the same. It is our place to keep these hills sacred." Lone Horn paused. "We must not allow settlers in, and we must keep Crow hunters out."

"What would you have us do?"

"The Crow are not without honor. I would prefer that they are turned away with the message never to return—" Lone Horn stopped mid-sentence and locked eyes, first with Anton, then with Eagle Feather Man. "If it is necessary, kill them, but do your best to leave one of them alive to go to their people and tell them what to expect if they ever return. Take seven men with you, take back what they have stolen, and thank them for their trouble before sending them away. Our people can use that food and the robes this winter."

* * *

Eagle Feather Man, followed by Anton, led the nine-person party strung out behind him. Eagle Feather Man knew the area, and Anton paid close attention to their surroundings, looking for landmarks he could use if he was ever in this area again. This particular valley was known to only a handful from the band of Lone Horn, and Eagle Feather Man knew of the abundant grasses that would attract and hold a few buffalo as the vast herds moved south to Nebraska Territory. There were few others that were aware of the area, and he was determined to keep it that way.

Walking in silence, Eagle Feather Man gestured to the others to hold their position. He signaled Anton to follow him to a crevasse. As Anton watched, his friend climbed between two vertical columns of rock by bracing his feet on each side of the opening and working his way to the flat slab at the top, where he motioned for Anton to follow. Minutes later the two of them lay on the flat surface thirty feet above the rest of the party waiting below.

Lying on his stomach, Anton watched as Eagle Feather Man crawled to the side overlooking the open valley and carefully squirmed to the edge. From where Anton was positioned, he had a clear view of the far side of the mile-wide stretch of open grassland. As he crawled forward to where Eagle Feather Man had stopped, more and more of the valley became visible.

There was nothing but open green grass—no buffalo, no hunters, and no sign that the buffalo had been there. He had almost reached the edge when he saw Eagle Feather Man jerk his head and back away from the edge.

"They're straight on the other side of this granite, and they are skinning two buffalo they must have shot recently. Let's get down." The two of them skidded down the opening much faster than they had climbed it.

"We go up to the two boulders," Eagle Feather Man pointed at two prominent rock formations about three hundred yards ahead that looked to be significantly above the elevation they now stood upon, "then we climb over and down the far side." The men looked among themselves, and excitement showed on every face.

Anton asked, "How close do you figure we'll be when we get to the flat land on the other side?"

"As I remember, we should have a cliff wall between them and us. We should be able to close to within twenty or thirty yards before we come into the open."

"You figure to give 'em a chance, or just open fire soon as we can?"

Eagle Feather Man's answer was immediate. "Lone Horn said to try to send 'em all back to the Yellowstone. If we have trouble, kill them all. Now let's move."

All nine of them jogged forward until they were below the two boulders.

"Now be careful, there's lots of loose rocks on the way to the top, and lots of 'em on the other side too. Watch your step. If we get them rolling down the far side, them Crow warriors is gonna hear us coming." Eagle Feather Man led the way to the top without incident.

On the way up, Anton realized for the first time that he was no longer a young man. Feeling every one of his sixty-eight years, he stepped aside to let the younger braves scamper up the incline. Upon reaching a cranny about fifteen yards from the top, he stopped to catch his breath.

Eagle Feather Man, ten or more years younger than Anton, came to his side. "Hard to walk on them round rocks, isn't it?"

"I'll say. I can feel the years in my legs. Was a time I'd scamper up this stuff like a cat. Afraid I can't do that anymore. Damn, this is a first for me." He rubbed his thighs.

Eagle Feather Man spoke. "I figure we need to have someone cover our back trail and block this here slope. It's the only way out of the flats unless you go a couple of miles south to where it dumps out on the plains. Them Crow likely know about it, and we don't want any of them getting through."

"Well, you better find one of the young braves to do that; we're gonna need my repeating rifle. If anyone misses their shot with them muskets, likely as not that one's gonna get away. Now let's get over this rise and do what we came to do."

With his rifle in his left hand, Anton stood and began to climb the short distance to the top, using his right arm to help maintain balance. Leaning on a granite protrusion, he planted his foot and stepped over a crevice. Without warning, the rock he was stepping on shifted and his foot dropped from under him. Feeling himself falling, he pushed off of the granite as he fought to stay upright.

The rocks shifted under his weight, and he knew he was going down. With his focus on protecting his rifle, he brought his left arm close to his body as his shoulder made contact with a massive abutment and his body twisted unnaturally. He felt his foot slide off another rock and jam in the crevice he was trying to avoid. Unable to stop his fall, his ankle turned while his foot was held tightly in place. The pain hit at the same moment he heard the bone snap.

In severe pain, Anton knew it was broken, yet he understood the importance of the mission they were on. Within moments, he was seated in a niche alongside the trail.

Eagle Feather Man had heard the fall and came quickly to his side.

Anton grimaced in pain. "My friend, take my rifle and leave me your musket. You must not let the hunters escape. I will wait here and make sure no one passes."

"Are you sure?"

"I am sure. Now go." Anton handed him his repeating rifle and held the musket as Eagle Feather Man worked his way over the ridge.

The minutes dragged by with no sound of fighting. Although the day was cool, Anton blinked away the sting of sweat from his eyes as the pain came and went in waves. Eagle Feather Man had placed him with his back against a downhill boulder, broken leg elevated toward the crest of the trail. With much effort, he forced the musket under his lower leg to act as a sort of splint, muzzle pointing toward the hill summit. The resultant support brought immediate relief.

The silence was broken by yells from the other side, followed by the discharge of firearms. More yelling, and Anton heard the *crack, crack, crack,* of his rifle. Then there was silence.

"Anton, one coming your way," Eagle Feather Man was yelling from far away, and only the acoustics of the open grassland and the granite cliffs carried the sound to him.

Realizing that he was stationary and without the power to move, he knew he must prepare for battle as best he could. His only weapon other than his knife was the musket he now used as a splint. As he inched the gun from under his leg and it began to offer less support, the agony was unbearable. He could pull it no farther. With both hands on the breech, he stopped to stabilize his leg and ease the anguish he felt.

It was at that moment he saw a hand appear at the summit and clasp onto a projecting boulder. As in a dream, the fingers tensed, seemingly under considerable pressure as another appeared, and slowly the space was filled, first by a forehead, then a full face, and finally by the upper torso of the Crow warrior.

As his body came into full view, his eyes darted from side to side, and then their eyes met. The warrior had a rawhide strap looped over his shoulder, allowing him full use of his hands while carrying his rifle on his back, barrel protruding upward. As he reached to swing it free, Anton yanked the musket free, jerked the hammer back with his thumb, and pulled the trigger.

As the shot echoed along the canyon walls, the warrior was bowled backward and out of sight on the far side of the rise. Anton, leg askew, felt like it was being crushed as his world grew dark and the musket fell from his hands.

* * *

They carried Anton by travois to the summer camp of Lone Horn, where he could be tended by Wakan Witshasha—Mystery Man. Star Woman was familiar with the power attached to the tribal healer, but her experience with the missionaries as a younger woman and knowledge of medicine as practiced at Fort Snelling in Minnesota instilled within her a skepticism regarding the medicine man's healing capabilities.

When Crazy Horse heard of the incident, he showed up at the camp to pay respects and offer to help in any way he could. Star Woman requested that he try to find Four Wings and tell him of the accident. The warrior left the camp the following morning to track down and retrieve Gentle Breeze and Four Wings.

Anton's treatment while in Lone Horn's camp failed to stretch the leg muscles sufficiently to set the break correctly. Although two stout branches served as the splint, it was clear to Star Woman that the leg had a definite bow.

After two weeks, her lack of faith in the medicine man came to the front, and she decided it would be best to take advantage of the physicians and techniques used by the whites. She took Anton to the Cheyenne River Agency. The agency was small and did not have a resident doctor, relying on a visiting surgeon every three weeks. As luck would have it, his next visit was in four days.

"Bring him in here; this'll have to do till the doc gets here." The agency quartermaster was the only officer there when they arrived. "This here room is set up for situations just like this."

Two young men from Lone Horn's band had traveled with Anton and Star Woman to help with the task of moving him and to act as protectors should it become necessary. After helping to get Anton settled on the small cot that served as a bed, they bade farewell and left to return to the hills.

"It feels much better on this bed." Anton rubbed the thigh on his broken leg. "This leg doesn't hurt as much when I drape the other off this cot. It is much better than lying flat on a blanket on the ground."

On the fourth day, around noon, the surgeon arrived at the agency. He was a lieutenant named Miller Pea. "That leg is badly damaged. Near's I can tell, if that bone heals at all, it's gonna have a serious bend to it," he said matter-of-factly. "There's two things we can do for your man. I can make an incision where the break occurred and take a look at what we've got; if all seems doable, get a couple of men and manipulate the leg to stretch the muscles and allow us to set the break so's the bone will grow back together. Ain't no guarantee that it won't kill him."

"That's it? What can you do for the pain? Something like that has to be excruciating."

"In the battlefield surgery tent, most passed out. We backed it up with opium when the patient stayed awake. A good share of them died."

"What's the second choice?"

"The second choice, and I'm glad you asked because this is the one I recommend, is to amputate that leg at the knee. Either way, he's gonna have one hell of a limp; there's less chance of infection and him losing his life if we remove the lower leg."

She stood in stunned silence. Her mind kept going over the words "remove the lower leg."

Her mind was flooded with memories of their years together. The first time she saw him; when he first saw her baby, Rising Eagle, and his explanation of how her husband, Tomawka, had died; Anton's kindness toward her and her son, and her growing appreciation, which turned into love; his kindness and solitary strength that set him apart from every other man; his patience while raising her son and his approval of Rising Eagle's vision quest, from which her son took the name Four Wings.

She had never heard a harsh word come from his mouth, and she remembered his pain at the death of Tatemina. How could he face the future with part of his body missing? Her mind churned as she mulled the choices. *No! You cannot take his leg! His life is better cut short than extended with the removal of his lower leg.*

Anton McAlister would not be tested with the amputation of his leg. She was confident of his choice in the matter; in fact, so much so that he would not be told of her decision.

"There is a third choice that you failed to mention." Now it was her turn to look directly into the surgeon's eyes. "Anton will heal as he lies. You will not make an incision, and you will not cause the pain of trying to reset the leg bone. All I ask is that he be allowed to remain here until the healing makes it possible for him to move with little or no pain."

CHAPTER FIFTEEN

White Poachers

With the sun just short of its zenith, Four Wings, Gentle Breeze, and Ogden Dent were almost clear of the hills as they moved west. Dent had traveled this route on his way into the hills, so he was leading the small party as they crested a rise overlooking a beautiful valley. It was cut down the middle by a stream that flowed from the high ground to their right, then down a slope populated by a mature stand of aspens. Where the aspen met the prairie grass of the valley, a small number of buffalo grazed.

"Have you ever seen anything as beautifully put together as this?" The wonder of the scene struck Gentle Breeze as she gazed upon it.

The three had stopped to take in the spectacular panorama lying before them. The open grassland stretched at least a mile. Although the September sun bathed the area, the golden leaves of the turning aspen twisted and turned in the occasional puffs of a gentle breeze that caressed the small valley. The picture it displayed was one of shimmering gold atop thin strings of milky silver that gave way to darkness as the stand deepened. Above and behind the golden sparkles, the hills were the deep green of the ponderosa pines; themselves topped with granite outcroppings that jutted into a clear, cobalt-blue sky.

"Beautiful, isn't it?" Four Wings spoke from behind.

Dent, sitting his horse in front of them, was awestruck as he inhaled the beauty of the moment. The three sat in silence as they examined what lay before them in minute detail.

Finally, Dent spoke, "It is easy to see the wonder of this place and the reason these hills are considered holy by the Sioux. I have a feeling that President Grant cannot offer nearly enough to pry it from their hands. The beauty is incomparable and beyond monetary value."

"Is there beauty in the mountains to the west that can compare to this?"

"I have learned from the Lakota that there is beauty in all things. What is more beautiful, the sound of a bull elk bugling or the call of the eagle? Is a newborn fawn as beautiful as a waterfall at the end of a valley? A freshly washed forest after a summer rain, or the beauty of the badlands at sunrise?"

He surveyed what lay ahead. "The beauty is there, as it is here. It is the beauty here that troubles me."

Suddenly, from the valley came the report of a rifle and one of the bison dropped where it stood. The three looked from one to the other. A second shot rang out, and another dropped. As the small herd began to mill in preparation to flee, simultaneous firing came from the tree line, and several more fell before the remaining buffalo thundered across the open ground away from the killing. Where the small herd once fed, now seven bison dead or dying were spread across a fifty-yard area.

As the three looked on in disbelief, four men walked from among the trees onto the open of the grassy plain.

Before Four Wings and Dent could react, Gentle Breeze urged her horse into a gallop down the swale leading into the meadow, directly toward the hunters.

Four Wings turned to his new friend. "I will go with her to learn who these men are. She is protecting her land. This is trouble! Work your way beyond them. They will expect nothing from that direction."

Without waiting for an answer, he put heels to the sides of his horse and charged after his wife.

The men had reached the first downed buffalo and were standing as a group, gesturing and congratulating each other on their brilliant marksmanship. The two riders charged unnoticed until they were almost on top of them, at which time they reined their mounts to a walk.

At their notice, the men's demeanor went from congratulatory to defensive, drawing back from the riders and spreading left and right.

Four Wings raised his right arm to indicate peaceful intent as they rode into the midst of the four. To one side lay the buffalo that had died with the first shot.

The men were white, and all looked with suspicion upon the riders.

"What the hell are you two doin' out here? That's a good way to get yerself kilt, ridin' in like that." The speaker had an air of superiority as he challenged them. "We're within our rights to be here, huntin' on this here land, so don't think about givin' us any shit."

He was of medium height and weight, but with two features that were noticeable: a long beard and hair that came below his shoulders. Both were red.

"We don't mean no harm. We was jest on ridge over there when we heard shooting and wondered maybe you could use help." Four Wings responded to Red Beard, intentionally butchering his diction, while his eyes surveyed the others.

Red Beard edged closer. "Well ain't this jest dandy, boys. This here Injun figures to help us out. What say we let 'em skin these buff and save us the trouble?" He exchanged looks with his closest mate.

Before Four Wings could move, one of the others was on him, grabbing hold of the buckskin on his left arm and pulling him from his horse. The fourth man pounced in the direction of Gentle Breeze, intending to do the same. She reined toward the oncoming man and drove forward, causing him to dive to one side as she charged past, hooves tossing soil into the air as she spun in the direction of the aspens.

* * *

The four men surrounded the lone Indian as he worked to skin the massive beast. The other six buffalo the men had killed lay to one side, ready for the same treatment.

Four Wings appeared intent on the work he was doing, seeing nothing beyond the job of skinning.

His face was battered; an untended cut on his left cheek had crusted over with blood, and his jaw was swollen to the extent that his left eye was nearly shut. Although his attention appeared to be on the animal, he knew his friends would attack, and he must be ready.

It happened in an instant. One of the men fell to the ground with an arrow protruding from his chest; moments later another staggered in a circle as blood erupted from his severed artery.

Four Wings moved with catlike speed. Before the man closest to him could react, he was taken to the ground, knife at his throat, and at the mercy of the Indian he had ridiculed while pummeling him with his fists minutes earlier.

Four Wings saw the man he thought of as Red Beard spin and run blindly toward the safety of the trees. Barely after he started his dash, an Indian stepped directly in front of him, blocking his path. Four Wings looked on in awe as he recognized the Indian as Crazy Horse.

Red Beard was holding his empy rifle like he would grip a club, both hands around the barrel. Crazy Horse had dropped his bow and stood ready with his knife, waiting for the white man to reach him.

While Four Wings maintained his dominion over the white man he had pinned to the ground, Red Beard darted to his right to avoid death at the hands of the Indian blocking his way. Within two strides, another body confronted him. Fear gripped Four Wings when he realized the body now blocking his path was that of Gentle Breeze. Without thought, he slammed his fist against the man's throat and growled, "If you move from here, you will die!"

Scrambling to his feet, he saw Red Beard lunge, rifle swinging in an arc intended to contact his wife's head. Incredibly, there was nothing but empty space where she once stood. Red Beard struggled to stop the momentum, causing him to stumble forward.

As Gentle Breeze spun to the side, Four Wings saw that she held a pole meant as part of a drying rack for the buffalo skins. Slamming the pole behind Red Beard's lead foot, it caught the shin of his trailing leg, and he went down hard, thrusting the barrel of his rifle forward to break his fall. Gentle Breeze swept the pole upward, maintaining contact, causing the man to drop his gun as he somersaulted. Instinctively, he extended his arm to break his fall. Four Wings saw his wrist bend at an awkward, unnatural angle. As the man crumbled, intense pain obvious on his face, he rolled to elevate his arm to relieve pressure on the wrist.

Gentle Breeze was on his chest in seconds, pinning him to the ground with the pole across his throat, cutting off his air supply. As he looked up from the ground, his eyes were filled with fear. In a desperate attempt to throw her off his chest, he arched his back and pushed his feet hard into the ground. His legs jerked and kicked and his arms swung wildly, wrist bending as that of a rag doll while his hand whipped and snapped to and fro as Gentle Breeze refused to be thrown off.

Then there was no movement.

"Gentle Breeze. It is over." Four Wings was standing behind her, legs straddling the now inert body upon which she sat holding the pole across his throat. "He is dead, it is over.

He placed his hands gently on her shoulders. "Gentle Breeze, it is over. He is dead. It is over, finished." He felt her soften, and the pole was released. She stood as he embraced her from behind. Turning in his arms, she collapsed as he held her tightly.

As Dent holstered his gun and approached, Four Wings saw Crazy Horse emerge from the aspens, raising his arm in greeting.

* * *

There was a short debate that centered on what to do with the remaining white hunter. After making him bury his friends, he was stripped naked and sent riding east to carry a warning to other white hunters: stay off Indian land.

Crazy Horse delivered the news of Anton's accident.

"It does not look good. I left them many days ago to find you. I feel Star Woman may need your help. The break is very bad."

With no forethought, Four Wings blurted, "Of course. We will return now."

Gentle Breeze said, "Yes, we could return now, but what of the hides and buffalo meat that is here? Our people need these things. Would you have us leave this for the animals?"

"May I offer a suggestion?" Ogden Dent stepped forward.

"Gentle Breeze and I will smoke this meat and scrape the hides. I figure three days ought to do it. When we finish, we will use the horses from the white hunters and bring the meat and hides back to Lone Horn's camp."

"That is a good plan, Owatumla." Gentle Breeze looked at her husband. "You ride with Crazy Horse, and we will follow after smoking the meat."

It was decided.

Before leaving, all helped prepare what they needed for stabilizing the meat and preventing it from spoiling. Two of them tied poles to act as a frame for the smoking hut while the other two cut the meat for smoking. The structure they built was much larger than the typical-sized enclosure used by the bands when several smaller huts were spread among families.

During this time, when all of them worked together to prepare to process the bounty of the buffalo, Four Wings's mind was with Anton and Star Woman. An injury like Anton's may eventually heal, but he had seen good men injured during a hunt, and although their bones healed, they never again loved their lives as before. Self-confidence seemed to erode, replaced with self-doubt. Their interactions with others became less cordial, and arguments between man and wife became commonplace. *Could this be in the future for Anton and Star Woman?*

Four Wings dismissed the thought. His whole life he had never heard a harsh word spoken between them. Each listened to the other, and the mutual respect they shared was impossible to overlook. They were his example, and he held them as his model for how he would live his life. He had followed his heart and found a woman he loved, a strong woman like his mother. For the first time, he found himself comparing his life to that of Anton and Star Woman, and he was satisfied.

Looking through the dead men's belongings, they found canvas that would be used to cover the frame and several other items used when on the trail for days at a time. All were taken; all would be brought back to Lone Horn's camp, including firearms and bullets.

When the camp had been set and Four Wings gathered deadwood for their fires, he watched the others as they worked together. They shared more than the labor; he found it obvious that they shared respect. Ogden Dent— Owatumla—had proven his friendship and concern for the people; Crazy

Horse hated the white men, yet here he was working hand in hand to achieve a common goal. And Gentle Breeze, the only woman he had ever met that was as strong as Star Woman, was his wife.

With plenty of deadwood for the fire, Four Wings and Crazy Horse bade farewell. With the sun well past its zenith, they rode south while Gentle Breeze and Dent went back to processing the meat into pieces suitable for smoking.

Four Wings's mind again returned to Anton's accident and how it may affect his future.

* * *

Upon reaching the camp of Lone Horn, the two warriors learned that Anton and Star Woman had stayed at the Cheyenne River Agency. Crazy Horse rode to rejoin his band, and Four Wings went to the agency.

Star Woman was outside at the water pump when he rode in. She paid little attention to the single rider that approached, focusing on the bucket she was filling. He dismounted and looped the reins over the hitching post and walked toward her. She turned, carrying the full bucket, and saw him as he moved in her direction. When realization hit that he was her son, she set the bucket on the ground and rushed to him. They embraced, each unwilling to release the other. Finally, she spoke.

"It is so good to see you, my son. Did Crazy Horse tell you of our accident?" She swiveled her head. "Where is Gentle Breeze?"

"She will be following in a couple of days. I will explain why she is not with me now. Where is Anton? I have heard that he has a very bad break. I understand it is his leg? Let us go to him, and I will explain what we have been doing since we left you."

"It is so good to have you here. Nothing has happened to Gentle Breeze, has it?"

"No, everything is fine. Will you take me to see Anton? Is he in much pain? I have worried about the two of you since I heard the news."

"He is strong. He will be pleased to see you now. We thought it possible that you would not be made aware."

The two of them stepped through the doorway into the small cabin.

"I'll be darned!"

Four Wings, eyes adjusting to the shadowy interior after coming from the bright sunlight, turned to the voice. There, much to his surprise, stood Anton.

"What? I thought you were hurt. Now I see you standing there. I had visions of seeing you pale as a sheet, lying in a pool of blood, breathing your last."

"Sorry to disappoint you." The smile on Anton's face showed his pleasure at being able to grab his son for support. "Where is Gentle Breeze?"

"That's the first thing I asked him too." Star Woman stepped closer to place her hands on both of the men. "Now tell us what has been happening. Where were you when you heard? Is all well with the two of you?"

"Things couldn't be better. Anton, you look much better than I expected. Crazy Horse made it sound like you were near death."

"Crazy Horse?" Anton said skeptically.

"Yes, Crazy Horse," Star Woman said. "He heard of your accident and came to offer his help. I asked him to find Four Wings."

"He is a good friend. He likely saved our lives." Four Wings was a little surprised at Anton's reaction to hearing that Crazy Horse had found them.

Anton quickly responded, "Of course he is a friend. I was surprised, that's all. His loyalty to the people makes him a fearsome adversary. I just thought—I guess it doesn't matter what I thought. You are here. That is good."

"It is good. We have missed you." Star Woman was feeling hopeful after experiencing long days of worry about both her son and her husband. "Anton is healing, and you are with us. My son, how I have missed you—we have missed you."

"Mother, Gentle Breeze will follow. I came as soon as I heard of Anton's injury." They sat and he continued, "We have met a man, a white man that lives with Lakota beyond the Bighorns. Gentle Breeze and this man, Ogden Dent, are preparing buffalo meat for the people. They will bring buffalo skins and much meat for Lone Horn's band."

He went on to explain how Dent came to be with them and the situation with the buffalo hunters as Anton and Star Woman listened.

Nine days later they were joined by Ogden Dent and Gentle Breeze.

CHAPTER SIXTEEN

Black Hills Gold

In July of 1874, the United States was into the second year of a depressed economy. On July 22, 1874, George Armstrong Custer led the 7th Calvary toward the Black Hills under the pretense allowed by the 1868 treaty for scouting for a fort location. The presence of prospectors as part of the company told the real reason behind the visit.

Four days later they were about twenty-five miles southwest of the Six Grandfathers on the edges of a fast-moving river called French Creek, deep into the hills, when they discovered paying quantities of placer gold.

The discovery made the papers, and miners flocked into the Black Hills to seek their fortunes in spite of the fact that the 1868 treaty banned all whites from the hills and committed the US government to expelling those that entered the area. The government did very little to put an end to the trespassing.

In the spring of 1875, Lone Horn led a delegation to Washington to seek relief from the incursions on Sioux land.

Upon hearing of the planned trip, Dent asked to be included, not as a representative of the native people, but as a citizen of the United States visiting his sister, Julia.

The delegation returned with nothing more than words from the government claiming insufficient manpower to stop the trespass.

Dent stayed in Washington when the chiefs returned to the Black Hills, not returning himself until autumn of that year. He met with Four Wings to explain what he had learned during his trip east.

"Grant wants me to work as a middleman in dealing with the non-treaty Sioux living on the unceded land. He figures I may have contacts that can help prevent more fighting."

"Far as I know, the Sioux are content and don't want to shed more of their blood. Them that's on the reservation don't want trouble. Neither do the non-treaty bands."

"There's more." Dent focused his eyes on nothing in particular and avoided making eye contact. "The government sent word late last winter telling the non-treaty bands to abandon the non-ceded land and report to the reservations. The weather prevented them from reaching all the bands, but that seems to make no difference. The notice delivered was more than a request. I've learned that every Indian living off the reservation is to be considered a hostile."

"What! How can that be?"

"Damned if I know, but there's even more bad news. Grant's military commanders responsible for enforcing the treaty, Sheridan and Crook, claim they can't keep the whites out of the Black Hills—too many prospectors, not enough troops. With the realization that there is gold in the hills, Grant is under pressure to get them under governmental control. He still figures he can buy the hills back."

Gentle Breeze, who had joined the two men, had heard what Dent said. "The people will never sell Pahá Sápa. Grant will have to take them by force."

"He claims he wants peace and is willing to pay a tidy sum and offer extra incentives to complete the purchase."

"They will not listen to him. The hills are sacred, and the game there is to be saved for when the buffalo move for the winter. My people will never agree to sell Pahá Sápa."

"I hope you are right. I told him I would try to speak with Sitting Bull, but I also told him that it would do no good."

* * *

Following the trip to Washington, Lone Horn's health began to deteriorate, and at the age of eighty-four, he died. His oldest son and successor, Spotted Elk, assumed the mantle of chief of the Miniconjou band. It was at this time that a trooper at the agency commented to the effect that he had big shoes to fill, and the name "Big Foot" was attached to him. From that point forward, he was known by that name to the whites.

With the passing of time, Anton's broken leg began to heal. He worked it hard to rebuild the muscle, although he could not avoid walking with a limp. Star Woman was thankful that he was still alive.

CHAPTER SEVENTEEN

The Rosebud

June 1876

Word was spreading through the camp that riders were approaching, and it appeared to be Crazy Horse and two others. Four Wings, excited at the prospect of seeing his friend again, walked to meet them.

"What has happened to bring you to our camp, my brother?"

"Have you heard that Sitting Bull is calling for warriors to meet at his camp on Rosebud Creek?" Crazy Horse dismounted.

Four Wings responded. "We have not heard this."

"We are told we must all move to reservation land. Those that remain off the reservation are to be considered hostile, and the government will send troops to force them to the reservations.

"They sent messengers during the cold months. Many camps never got the word. The government has begun their task of rounding up the people. Sitting Bull has called for all warriors to gather at his camp on the Rosebud to counsel together." Crazy Horse spoke with disdain.

Four Wings said nothing of what Dent had told him about his meeting with Grant.

Crazy Horse continued, "I would like you to ride with me to the Rosebud. We will hear what Sitting Bull has to say."

"I must speak to Gentle Breeze about this. Please join us. We will feast to our good fortune in meeting again."

"I will not hear words discouraging us from fighting. Your woman will not want you to join me, and although Anton is a great warrior, he does not wish to carry the fight to the whites. I will camp in the pines." He pointed to a distant hill bristling with ponderosa pine trees. "Join me there before the moon goes behind the pines, and we will ride together."

* * *

"Of course I do not want you to go there," Gentle Breeze said angrily. The conversation had been going on for nearly an hour. "If you fight the white man, you will die. As sure as we stand here now, you will die; if not in battle, you will die by hanging. Do not do this thing."

He held her eyes fast without saying a word.

Star Woman spoke her final words on the matter. "You saw what happened in Minnesota. If that is what you want, it is your decision. I can see no benefit in joining in another war against the whites—and make no mistake about it, that is exactly where this is heading."

"I have no intention of fighting a war. I only wish to offer support to my friend and to learn what Sitting Bull would have the people do. He is a man of peace, a holy man concerned for his people."

Four Wings turned to face Anton, sitting to his left.

"I see the unfairness. I feel empty inside at the prospects of another war that we cannot win." Anton placed his hands on the young man's shoulders. "I say go, hear what is said. Reflect on your future, our future, the future of the Sioux nation. Then decide if your death will make a difference in another war. I say your death will do nothing to preserve our way of life, but your living means there is a chance for all of us. It is through your life that you may affect the future; you will have an active part of what lies ahead." He looked deeply into the dark eyes before him, holding his gaze. "You must follow your heart; it will guide you."

A single tear ran down the older man's cheek as they embraced.

Before the moon dropped behind the distant tree line, Four Wings rode from camp to meet Crazy Horse. His mind was a jumbled mess, bouncing from the noble act of protecting a way of life, then returning to a specific memory—one that came uninvited when he considered battle in an all-out war. He saw the eyes of the warriors as they butchered the dead at Fort Phil Kearney when they defeated the US Army during Red Cloud's War.

He had seen good when he was young; Anton and Star Woman had faith in human motives; they lived with whites and counted them as friends. But he saw the injustices, heard the lies from the white men. Was Crazy Horse right? All whites were the enemy of the Sioux?

* * *

June 12, 1876

In response to Sitting Bull's call, many Sioux, Arapaho, and Cheyenne warriors were joining him at his camp. Crazy Horse, Four Wings, and two others had ridden northwest. The weather was hot. The sun baked the skin as the breeze—itself hot—did nothing to bring relief. As the sun inched its way toward the western horizon, the air slowly began to cool.

As they grew closer to the main camp, they saw hundreds that were doing the same. Sioux and Cheyenne warriors, women, and even children crossed in front of them, some arriving, and some departing. In the distance, more were approaching from other directions.

It was well after dark when they entered the camp. Crazy Horse located Sitting Bull and introduced Four Wings. The greeting was terse as the great chief was preparing himself for a sun dance ritual in hopes of gaining power and good fortune for what lay ahead.

Four Wings and Crazy Horse found a space where they could camp for the night. After walking the camp area, Four Wings felt a tug of ambivalence as he viewed the wild eyes and determined faces of the warriors. This was something he had never before experienced, and it caused a shiver that ran the length of his spine. He spent the night in solitude as his mind raced and indecision filled him as he thought about his future.

As the darkness gave way to red-cotton skies harkening a sun-filled dawn, Sitting Bull began the ritual by leading others in the dance. They sang and offered prayers to Wakan Tanka—the Great Spirit. Four Wings sat and watched as Crazy Horse joined the dance alongside a Hunkpapa chief named Gall he knew from the sporting matches.

After dancing for several hours, Crazy Horse and Gall sat to one side. They had slaked their thirst and were now discussing the battles that were bound to occur. Four Wings had joined them and reacquainted himself with Chief Gall.

The men discussed the potential for another war with the whites. Gall told them that many soldiers were moving west, some from the north and some from the south. He thought they intended to eliminate the non-treaty Sioux once and for all.

"A chief named Crook has many men, and they have much firepower. He comes to destroy the people. We would be smart to pick our battle location to attack him when he doesn't expect it."

"What you say holds much promise for our people if we can bring the fight to him at a time and place of our choosing. The scouts say he has a large force, nearly a thousand men."

As they spoke, the respected leader Sitting Bull continued to dance.

The men sat silently for several minutes, during which Four Wings considered the views expressed by Gall. Such action would undoubtedly bring a war to the people, and he feared the outcome. Finally, Crazy Horse spoke. "We will speak with Sitting Bull and see what he says on the matter."

Sitting Bull danced for forty-eight hours without food or drink, having fifty cuts delivered on each arm as a sign of sacrifice. Near the end of the second day, he collapsed. The following day, Four Wings, unaccustomed to long celebrations, had very little rest and was almost asleep on his feet, but he went with the two men to find Sitting Bull. The holy man was awake in his tipi enjoying some herbal tea when the warriors came to him. He bade them to enter.

Before they could open the conversation, Sitting Bull made a proclamation, "I had a vision during the dance, a vision that bodes well for the people." He took a sip from the hollow gourd holding his tea. His visitors sat patiently while the respected leader searched his inner-self. After several minutes, he continued.

"I saw soldiers on horseback falling from the sky. They were falling upside down, and their hats were falling off. They fell to the ground like grasshoppers. And I heard a voice say, 'I give these to you because they have no ears.'"

The three warriors sat with Sitting Bull for a long time as each watched the small fire burn out inside the chief's tipi. There were occasional words spoken, but each appeared to be searching inside themselves for truths about what could happen in the coming days.

Four Wings, torn between the two worlds in which he existed, sought to understand what the future would bring. His friend Crazy Horse would fight to live as before; Ogden Dent had learned that Grant intended to take the Black Hills. What better way than to force a war? He had seen what happened in Minnesota in '62—families ripped apart, people that once called each other friend became enemies.

His adoptive father, Anton, had recently told him to follow his heart. Dent, Gentle Breeze, and he had talked about this.

There was little time. As the three warriors left the tipi, he knew what he must do. He spoke to Crazy Horse and explained his intent, and while the leader expressed regret at the decision made by the younger Four Wings, he honored his decision, and they parted as brothers.

* * *

Four Wings had returned from the Rosebud a few hours earlier. Gentle Breeze, Four Wings, and Ogden Dent were gathered together in the small building on the agency called home by Anton and Star Woman. The setting was casual, but the agenda was clear to Four Wings. He had brought them all together to convince Anton and Star Woman that a move from the Black Hills would be in their best interests.

The conversation began with the men discussing the potential for another war with the whites. Anton told them that he knew many soldiers were moving west. Four Wings was alarmed that, like Gall, Anton thought they intended to eliminate the non-treaty Sioux once and for all.

During a break in the conversation, Gentle Breeze saw the opening for them to discuss leaving the hills, and she intended to draw Dent into it. It was paramount that he tell the others of Grant's plan to eliminate the non-treaty Indians.

"I would like to talk." It was somewhat irregular for a woman to join the warriors in a conversation such as this. But the two women present had earned the respect of the men, and there was no opposition. "We have heard of a plot to take Pahá Sápa from the people. President Grant talks of peace while planning for war."

There was a stunned silence until Anton spoke. "We have seen this happen many times when treaties are set aside and less favorable treaties are proposed. There are stories upon stories—many false. How is it that you learned of this? Why would we believe it?"

"Our friend here," she gestured toward Dent, "knows the president's plans."

All present turned their eyes to the white man.

Dent responded, "First, let me say, my heart is that of a Sioux. My skin is white, but I have taken the ways of the Indian. I have lived in friendship with them for many years. More than once, they saved my life. This man and woman," he gestured to Four Wings and Gentle Breeze, "saved my life when all hope was lost. I owe them my loyalty. I give them my friendship and my love."

Gentle Breeze, knowing that Dent tended to drift off subject, steered the conversation back to her objective.

"This man has had tea with the president. He knows him well." She met his eyes.

Dent took his cue. "To make a long story short, my sister is married to him. I knew him when he was a common man, but rest assured, my sister is President Grant's wife."

Hearing this for the first time, Anton and Star Woman were shocked.

"I came west nearly twenty years ago after a disagreement with our father about slavery. My sister, Julia, met Grant through my brother. They were classmates at military school. Grant and my sister married. Familiar with my life in the mountains, Grant asked me to explore the mindset of the Sioux regarding selling the Black Hills to the government. It was during that task that I almost lost my life and I learned that Pahá Sápa would never be sold. I sent a message telling him that.

"A short time ago, Julia bade me come to Washington to discuss important things with Grant. That is when I went there with Red Cloud and the others." Dent rose from his seated position and began to pace.

"It turns out that he wanted me to find Sitting Bull and other influential chiefs and try to convince them that the millions offered would care for the Sioux Nation for the next generation." His voice began to rise in volume as he continued to speak.

"He convened a grand council, and when Crazy Horse and Sitting Bull failed to participate, he sent a messenger to Sitting Bull's camp. I was with that messenger. The task was to convince the chief to consider selling the Black Hills.

"As I watched, Sitting Bull picked up a handful of dirt and, stirring it with his thumb, let it fall through his fingers and said, 'I do not want to sell or lease any land to the government—not even as much as this.' At that moment, it became clear in my mind why the people followed this man."

"We know the government wants the hills," Anton said. "I haven't heard anything that could ever make the people consider selling."

"The government intends to take them by force."

Anton was speechless; his eyes registered disbelief. Opening wide, they began to narrow as he tilted his head to one side. "Now how can that happen without a great outcry from the people? We have honored the 1868 treaty."

"Do you see the flow of prospectors into the hills? Do you see any attempt by the army to stem that flow? The answer is no. The situation is made worse by the government's insistence on clearing the non-treaty Indians from the non-ceded lands to the west." He stopped his pacing and turned to the center of the room. "He intends to force the Sioux to fight for what is theirs, and when he moves against us, he can sell the move to the press—and Congress—as a retaliatory action."

There was dead quiet in the room.

Gentle Breeze faced Anton and Star Woman. "You must come with us to the north. There are many Sioux there now. They will welcome us."

CHAPTER EIGHTEEN

Into Canada

On the morning of June 20, 1876, the five of them rode north from the agency as the eastern sky began to show the aura of dawn on the prairie. The weather was calm, and the temperature was pleasantly cool. That would change when the sun broke over the horizon.

Gentle Breeze led the others as they headed northwest. Her familiarity with the land north of the Cheyenne River made her the obvious choice to lead the way. They planned to ride until their bodies told them they must stop for sleep. They carried dried buffalo meat to eat on the trail, and each person had their separate cache of water.

On the third day, they rode through an area peppered with depressions holding groundwater runoff and the occasional freshwater spring. Pure luck placed them in a swale, the lowest part of which was filled with tall swamp grasses.

Star Woman was the first to hear the sound of shod hooves striking sandstone as riders approached from the east. Alerting the others, they concealed themselves in the tallest reeds, hoping to go unnoticed by the horsemen. With the unrest and building tension between the army and the Lakota, they thought it best to avoid being seen.

Moments after they first heard them, the riders crested the rolling hill southeast of where they hid. Two columns of cavalry rode in a westerly direction. The most striking thing was the total number of riders that rode by their hiding place. It took nearly a half hour for them to pass from the first rider to the last. Trailing the troopers were wagons filled with supplies, and bringing up the rear were three field cannons.

"This doesn't look good." Anton was between the two women, but his comment was directed at Dent. "Do you suppose this is the start of what you said was going to happen? Is this Grant's first move to take the hills?"

"Something else must have happened; he wouldn't move on the hills before it was apparent that the Indians were starting the fight. By the number of men we just saw go past and the cannons and supplies, it sure looks like something has happened. They look to be headed west to the Powder River basin rather than into the Black Hills."

* * *

Not far from where they hid, a man lay on the top of a high cliff face, stomach down, fingers twisting a calibration knurl until the eyepiece presented a clear image of the approaching riders. He was doing what he did every morning when the sky was clear and the day lay in front of him. He had noticed the considerable dust cloud long before they came into view. As they emerged, cresting a distant hill, the army telescope he used showed a column of cavalry riders that seemed to have no end.

Approximately five minutes from where he lay was a narrow cave entrance that opened into a larger area completely hidden from the outside world. It was where Arnold Quarterman called home, and from the top of the vertical butte, he could see miles in every direction. Since losing his horse a year ago after the animal's leg was broken trying to traverse rock-strewn, rugged country, Arnold had grown comfortable living completely alone. The sparse trees growing among the butte crevasses provided firewood, and a nearby spring less than a quarter mile east of the cave provided water.

The horse had provided Arnold's sustenance the previous winter, after which the occasional traveler provided his nourishment.

Of necessity, Arnold began to view humans as another game animal, and he became a predator, prone to eating human flesh. As his solitary existence impacted him with ever deepening madness, his mind was unpredictable chaos, and his conversations with himself grew dark.

He grabbed the telescope and steadied it, elbows on his knees, and twisted the calibration knurl again.

* * *

Gentle Wind led the riders as they crested the far side of the depression in which they had hidden from the cavalry. The sun was at their backs when she noticed a reflection that appeared on the top of a distant butte. She spoke to Four Wings, who was riding on her right side.

"I just saw a flash from the top of that butte. It wasn't natural."

"You talking about the one way up ahead?"

"Yes, look at the highest one, just about the middle . . . look—there. I just saw it again."

Four Wings had seen the flash the second time. "Yes, I saw that one; there it is again. It looks like someone's signaling with a mirror."

He turned to Dent. "Whoever is up there doesn't seem to be trying to be invisible. Whoever it is looks to be close to the ground on the top of that butte. What do you think?"

His answer came quickly. "I think we keep riding like we don't see a thing. I don't know what it means, but it's for sure a reflection off of something." He rode as though there was nothing unusual but spoke to Anton, who was close behind.

"Anton, see that light on the top of that butte yonder?"

"I been seeing it for a little while; I think I know what it is." Urging his mount to come alongside Four Wings, he said, "Looks to me like the sun reflecting off a piece of glass. I've seen something like that before, and I figure someone is watching us through a telescope. Everyone just keep riding until we decide what to do. "

They advanced a good hundred yards while they considered the threat. "This is what we're gonna do, " Four Wings said. "The first depression we come to that we think is deep enough, I'm gonna peel off to the west while we're still in sight of the top of that butte. Once I get out of sight, I'm gonna dismount and walk the opposite direction while hidden by the rise." His mind raced as he spoke, not at all confident that this plan would work but unable to conjure an alternative.

"The four of you keep on this here trail while I mount up and circle to the backside of that bluff. Best case is I locate him before anything happens; worst case is he gets off a shot." Four Wings looked directly at Dent. "I'd sure like it if you would ride closest to the trouble side."

"It would be my honor."

* * *

Dent was leading the others toward where the trail narrowed before opening to the prairie beyond. "I'm thinking this cut ahead is dangerous. I wonder if Four Wings has circled it yet."

"It's tough to say. Could be he's already on the other side, or it could be he's had to take a wide path around." Anton shared Dent's apprehension. "What do you think about dropping off this here trail and settling in for a bit to give him more time?"

"It makes sense. If you can find a spot, I will see if there is another way past this place. I just don't like the looks of what's ahead."

The group turned aside and settled into a bowl about a hundred yards west of the butte. Out of sight from the bluff, Dent quietly left them to circle yet farther from the high ground.

* * *

Four Wings, having skirted to the backside of the butte, had tied his horse to a scrubby bush and was staring at the wall, nearly forty feet high. It was the only place that gave him any chance to reach the top. With a rawhide strap over his shoulder and across his chest, he slipped his rifle on his back and started the climb. The first twenty or so feet consisted of a boulder field caused by pieces breaking away in the past and creating a landslide that crashed down, carrying rock and limestone pieces to the bottom. After working his way over the boulder field, he climbed inside vertical voids and the splits in the butte face, seeking handholds to pull himself upward.

Now at the top, he searched every nook and cranny with his eyes before advancing the few feet to find cover behind one of the sparse bushes. Although it looked flat from below, the head of the butte was a dome, with the center of the area a good five feet higher than the surrounding terrain. The surface across the full top was filled with cracks in the sandstone, from which grew small cactus plants and the occasional scrubby bush. It was the infrequent bush he used for cover as he advanced. Scampering as low to the ground as he could, he moved forward bush by bush, taking several minutes at every stop to scan the area all around before moving on. He wasn't sure how long he had been crouching, but it was long enough that he began to feel his legs start to cramp from the effort.

Slowly, very slowly, he began to straighten, head and upper body turning to take in the area around him. There was nothing. The top of the butte was empty. Then he saw him. The figure lying near the edge was inching forward. Something wasn't right; he looked for another person, examining every inch that was visible and seeing no trace of anyone else, he called to the child lying near the edge of the cliff face.

"Hey, boy!"

The childlike figure pulled the trigger. The discharge was deafening, and the man in his sights on the ground below was bowled over. As the boy ratcheted the lever on his rifle to expel the old and load a new cartridge into the chamber, Four Wings struggled to understand what he was seeing. As the small body twisted and the rifle barrel arced in his direction, he instinctively ducked to one side and heard the discharge and the bullet whined as it passed to the left of his ear. As he watched, the face of the shooter came into clear view. Tangled, shoulder-length hair and unkempt whiskers framed eyes that were like lightning bolts blasting forth from the deranged mind behind them. Mesmerized by the sight, Four Wings watched as the boy rolled while cocking his rifle for another shot. But he was too close to the edge, and it seemed to be in slow-motion as his upper torso slipped over and disappeared from view, the sound of his rifle echoing off the butte face as it clattered its way to the bottom.

Four Wings yelled from where he crouched on the top of the butte. "Hello, below! Did anyone get hit when he shot?"

Dent yelled, "I saw Anton go down!"

Four Wings felt a shudder pass through his body at hearing that Anton had been hit. "I'm going to find the way down. I'll be there as soon as I can."

He cleared the bushes and saw a spot where three boulders converged on the surface of the butte. He walked in that direction until he saw the opening they sheltered. *I wonder if this cave will take me to the bottom.* Viewing the possibility of avoiding the dangers he faced while scaling the wall to reach the top, he entered the breach and saw that it opened above and appeared to be a natural chimney angling downward. The open pathway was flooded with light.

This looks like a good way down. He used the strap and slung his rifle over his shoulder and began the descent. The angle was such that he backed down the incline, belly down, sliding his feet while maintaining contact with his hands as he descended feet first.

While near the top, he thought there was an unusual odor. The farther he went, the stronger the odor became, and by the time he backed into an open void the stench was unbearable. Pulling his shirt up to cover his nose, he looked around to find that he was in a large cave. It looked like a tunnel left the far side of the room in which he now stood, and in a nook in the solid rock about forty feet away he saw red cloth bundles stacked on the rock floor. About halfway between the bundles and where he stood, there was a circle of smaller rocks, the center of which held partially burned sticks over a thick heap of ashes. On one side was a kettle, its outside surface blackened by the fire.

The stink was overwhelming, and he brought his forearm across his face to help block the smell. He walked toward the bundles and realized what he was looking at.

The bundles were piles of rotting hair, with pieces of bone jutting here and there. Beyond the hair piles, he saw a partially rotted face on a human skull, hacked open, bloody, matted hair covering decomposing flesh.

He turned away and, pulling his shirt away from his face, dropped to his knees as his stomach turned inside out. He retched, wave after wave. When it finally stopped, he got to his feet and staggered toward the opening he hoped would lead him out of this hell.

* * *

It was nearly an hour before Four Wings, drenched in sweat, joined the others. Much to his surprise and great relief, Anton was sitting on a large piece of sandstone, back leaning against the trunk of a scrubby cedar. Four Wings saw that someone had retrieved his horse.

Gentle Breeze ran to him with Star Woman close behind. Both women embraced him as though he had been gone for months.

Dent spoke first, "When I saw Anton go down, I figured it was over. Anybody hit like you looked to be hit ain't getting up." He looked at Anton.

"What happened? It looks like you weren't touched." Four Wings didn't understand.

Anton, a satisfied look on his face, bent and picked his rifle off the ground. "Look at this." He held it out as evidence of the reason he was unscathed. The place where the barrel connected to the action was bent inward, rendering the firearm unusable.

He shook his head in disbelief at what he was saying. "I was holding this thing in front of me. That bullet caught the widest part of the gun that was laying against my chest." He rubbed his fingers over the impact point. "I ain't supposed to be alive. If it hadn't been for your shot that took him down, we'd all be dead by now—at least the women and me."

Four Wings replied, "I didn't fire my rifle."

Silence prevailed. "I was looking at this kid, and he rolled over and took a shot at me. The recoil musta pushed him over the edge. All I did was give him a yell." He looked around. "Did any of you look at the body?"

"I checked to make sure he was dead," Dent said. "Ain't nobody could have lived after that fall. His arm was wedged up behind his head, and he was a bloody mess. All I saw was a dainty-looking man with long hair and lots of whiskers."

Four Wings looked in the direction of the cave he had discovered. "I think we've seen him before." He shifted his gaze between Star Woman and Anton.

"Remember when we were on the prairie after the hangings in Minnesota when we were just coming west?" The two nodded.

"Remember the kid with the repeating rifle? That little man Anton thought was a child is the same person that lies dead at the base of that hill. I'd bet my life on it."

"What?" Anton was taken aback.

Four Wings continued, "I found the way he used to get to the top. It goes through a cave about thirty feet up. The cave has a natural chimney. That's how I came down." He wiped his hands over his face. "The first thing that hit me was the smell of rotting flesh." He paused to exhale. "Inside that cave were scalps and entire heads just laying there rotting." He felt the bile beginning to rise again. Gentle Breeze moved to embrace him as he choked up, unable to go on.

The reign of terror unleashed by Arnold Quarterman had come to an end.

* * *

Two days later, they were riding on an open plain without definable characteristics when they came across a well-traveled road, wagon tracks rutted into its surface. In the distance was a marker of sorts that looked to be a sign.

Dent, riding to the left of the others and the closest to the marker, reined his horse to a standstill.

"I'm going to ride over there and see what this is all about. Be back in no time." The others watched as he put his heels to the horse's flanks and galloped down the well-worn track. Without stopping, he slowed his horse to a walk and circled the sign, then rode straight back.

"Well, we've made it to Canada. That was a sign that had a painted arrow and the words New Town."

"Do you know that town?"

"No, I've never heard of that town, but the name is written in French." Ogden Dent and Star Woman were the only two of the five that spoke French; Dent as a result of his education, Star Woman because of her years in Minnesota dealing with French fur traders and her time spent helping to translate the Bible from French into the Dakota language.

They turned their horses west, the direction the arrow pointed, and a short time later saw the buildings of a small village appear on the horizon. Entering the settlement, the realization that they were now on Canadian soil sank in. There was no longer a need to travel with extreme caution.

Dent had made inquiries while with his sister and learned that a significant number of Dakota had settled in an area called Wood Mountain, a short distance north of the Montana/Canada border. They learned that the settlement they sought lay a day's travel to the northwest.

Without hesitation, they continued west and completed their journey, arriving at Wood Mountain the following midday. Dent searched until he located Eyes Of Wolf, a Lakota friend from the mountains of Montana that he knew had come to this place, and the five were welcomed to settle in with the small band under his leadership.

* * *

They had barely settled in when Bloody Moon, one of the men that was with Anton and Many Feathers when Anton broke his leg, rode into camp with news.

From him, they heard of the battles that had taken place while they were on the trail. Crazy Horse had attacked the army at Rosebud Creek. It was clear to Four Wings that his friend had carried out the plan that he and Gall had discussed while he was with them.

"Crazy Horse pulled his warriors back from the Rosebud and joined the camp of Sitting Bull at the Little Bighorn River." Bloody Moon's pride shone as he spoke. "The camp was large, and the warriors wanted to fight." His eyes were alive. "Yellow Hair made the mistake of opening the battle. Our people fought well. The fight, from beginning to end, lasted only a short time. The people defeated the army at the Greasy Grass, and we knew we must spread ourselves on the land to avoid more soldiers. Sitting Bull led his people away from there. He now moves to avoid contact with the army and hunts as before. Crazy Horse and many young warriors went to the Yellowstone Country where they can evade the army. It is there that they will live."

"What of all the others that camped with Sitting Bull? There were many at the Greasy Grass."

"Many families were moved to the reservations, where they were told they will be cared for. They will join those already there."

* * *

The following months went by very fast. Ogden Dent spent considerable time with friends he had made when living near the Bighorns while Four Wings and Anton worked on building sturdy log cabins. The Canadian Mounted Police, not entirely comfortable with the situation, set an outpost near where the Indians settled and watched the comings and goings in the various camps as there were occasional complaints from whites in the area regarding issues of trespass and theft.

Sitting Bull Arrives

On February 28, 1877, the Manypenny Agreement annexed Sioux land and identified separate agencies to which the people must report. This agreement followed the discovery of gold, and abrogated the treaty signed at Fort Laramie in 1868 that had established the Great Sioux Reservation, by taking back the Black Hills from the Sioux.

The army continued to harass the Indians to force them to accept reservation life. With the shortage of game, constant pressure from the army, and ceaseless travel to avoid contact, one by one and nearing starvation, the non-reservation chiefs registered at the various agencies and relegated their bands to life on the reservation, where they were promised food and allowed to live as it pleased them.

Meanwhile, Sitting Bull continued to avoid contact with the army as much as possible, constantly on the move. Finally, nearly a year after the Battle of Little Bighorn, on May 5, 1877, he set out to lead his people to Canada, where they could continue to live as they had for centuries.

* * *

There was great excitement spreading among the people. Word had been delivered that morning from an advance scout that Sitting Bull was crossing into Canada and expected to arrive that evening with his band of warriors and their families.

"This is good." Gentle Breeze felt the excitement rising within their camp. "We can learn of the happenings in our homeland. He will have much to tell, and we will have much to learn."

Star Woman said, "Do not expect good things, young one. I fear the worst has happened."

Anton added, "Things cannot be good with the people. Sitting Bull would not come here unless he was driven here. The soldiers we hid from on our journey were heading into the Powder River country where Sitting Bull ranged. They have driven him out—this is not good."

* * *

Sitting Bull's entrance into the Lakota camp was triumphant and did much to buoy the spirits of the weary band. Much was made of their journey and avoidance of contacting the army on the way. Many in Sitting Bull's band had relatives in the Lakota camp of Eyes of Wolf and had not seen them since 1875, when they moved from the mountains west of the Little Bighorns. For the first time in many months, Sitting Bull's band set their tipis in anticipation of being in one place for a long time.

Sitting Bull remembered Four Wings from the meeting in his camp on Rosebud Creek, and the two found agreement on most things. As the two men talked from time to time, the difference between Sitting Bull and Crazy Horse became more and more obvious to Four Wings. Sitting Bull was a holy man. He fought only to preserve his people, killing only when protecting them, much preferring to settle disputes with words rather than force. Crazy Horse was a warrior. His first instinct was to fight when faced with a confrontation, and he was good at it.

Sitting Bull now shared a fire in the cabin Four Wings had built for Gentle Breeze and himself. Sitting Bull said, "Crazy Horse led his warriors well at Rosebud. General Crook hid behind his Crow and Shoshoni allies." Disgust was in his voice. "Without them, he would have seen much trouble. We lost few men, as did Crook. Crazy Horse pulled his warriors back, leaving Crook on the battlefield, giving the appearance that he was the victor. Only later was the success of the raid on the Rosebud made evident when Crook did not fight at the Greasy Grass."

"We have heard about the Little Bighorn battle, and the people are stirred. It is like the vision you described when we shared your tipi. It was as you said; the Greasy Grass fight saw the soldiers fall as you described."

Sitting Bull nodded. Four Wings continued, "Have you heard news of Crazy Horse?"

"I know what others know. In the Yellowstone country, he tires of running from the army. His people are tired of staying one step ahead of battle. The government offers safety on the reservation. They tell stories of contentment by the reservation Indians; I am told they went so far as to promise Crazy Horse his own agency. I am told he has moved his people to the Red Cloud Agency near Fort Robinson."

"Has this already happened? Is he now under control of the army?"

"He is on the reservation and has made a pledge to not fight again."

CHAPTER TWENTY

South Again

"I have heard that Crazy Horse has turned himself into the authorities and is now near Fort Robinson waiting for an agency to be built for him on reservation land," Four Wings told Dent. "They have promised him safety. I will visit him where is. I will see for myself how this reservation life agrees with him. His hatred for the whites is strong. I fear for what he might do."

Dent was quick to reply. "I will ride with you—not to guarantee your safety, but it can do no harm. If all goes well, we will be on reservation land in two days."

The two men left Wood Mountain the following morning as the sun broke the horizon. Their time on the trail was without incident, and they reached the Cheyenne River Agency. In a short time, they were seated in Spotted Elk's house, built for him by the government.

Spotted Elk said, "It is good to see my friends after this time apart. Is everyone well at Wood Mountain?"

Four Wings replied, "We are well. Gentle Breeze is angry at losing the hills, but she is beginning to accept what has happened. My family and I have seen the government take our land before, and it is difficult to watch it happen here." He paused, then continued, "Star Woman is strong and will withstand much; Anton understands and, as always, seems to accept the inevitable. However, his leg is not good."

Dent was quiet in the background, listening as the two men talked.

"I have missed Crazy Horse and wish to refresh myself in his company. I thought you could send me to his camp."

Spotted Elk seemed surprised. "There is much army between here and his camp. Those that they know the army does not bother, but they often detain those they do not know."

Dent spoke up. "That is why I am here. They will not detain us." Over time, he had learned that the blue officer's jacket given him by President Grant allowed him access to forts and army camps while his charisma caused him never to be challenged by the authorities. Since his meeting with the president, he had been able to acquire army tack for his horse, rendering his presence that of a legitimate army officer. His bravado allowed him to pass as one on a "special assignment" by the president of the United States.

"This is good." Spotted Elk then told the two men precisely where they would find the warrior. After all was settled, Spotted Elk became serious. "There is some news that is not good." He had picked a small branch off the kindling near his fireplace hearth and began to peel the dried bark while the two patiently waited for him to speak. "Eagle Feather Man has gone before us."

"You mean he has died?" Four Wings felt a pressure building within his chest, and it became difficult to draw a breath.

"During his move from the hills, members of the cavalry responsible for escorting his band to a new location thought it great sport to shoot at the eagle while he hunted."

"Oh no!"

"They killed it, and Eagle Feather Man attacked the trooper that had done the shooting. He was killed moments later."

"Them sons-a-bitches." Four Wings's face flushed as anger overtook him.

He went strangely silent as he sat for a long time. His mind recounted his relationship with the father of his wife, a man who had much to live for and one that loved his daughter more than life itself. His pride of her and his pride of having the eagle that hunted only for him was evident to all. Four

Wings knew that his gift of the eagle was known far and wide and drew respect from all the bands. *How will I tell Gentle Breeze that her father has been killed?*

Finally, he stood and walked to the door and exited, followed closely by the others. Mechanically placing one foot in front of the other, he continued walking toward his horse. Reaching out, he gripped the reins in his left hand, grabbed her mane with the same, and swung himself onto her back. "Them dirty bastards."

Dent and Spotted Elk reached out and exchanged forearm grips, Dent mounted, and the two urged their horses forward.

* * *

It was the time of the new moon in May of '77. There was minimal talk as they rode with purpose, arriving at the camp of Crazy Horse as the eastern sky began to lighten. They had encountered no army during the entire night's ride.

Crazy Horse had bathed in the stream near his tipi and was talking with his cousin, Touch The Clouds, son of Lone Horn and brother of Spotted Elk, when the two riders approached. They exchanged greetings, and all entered his tipi.

After exchanging pleasantries and a conversation that brought his guests up-to-date, Crazy Horse stated, "You must not stay here, my friend. It is dangerous. There are those within us that seek favor with the army and do so by stirring trouble."

"You have many loyal warriors; how is it that members of your band bring you trouble?" Four Wings was concerned.

Crazy Horse motioned to Touch The Clouds. "We were talking about that when you rode in. My cousin is loyal, while many others plot for the white man's favor. I do not know who I can trust here. The army has others watching me at all times."

He directed a question to his cousin. "Do you know those who are trustworthy?"

Touch The Clouds thought before replying. "I know your friend He Dog can be trusted. I also think Little Big Man, your friend for many years, remains true. I will watch very closely and warn of those you must be wary of." Turning to address the two new arrivals, he continued.

"The army has appointed men as reservation police. They are to keep the peace and tell of troublemakers. They are not always honest. We have many that wish to accuse others to gain favor with the army. It is difficult to understand who can be trusted."

Four Wings answered. "I understand. Have you thought of coming to Canada? There are many Lakota that live there now."

Crazy Horse answered quickly. "We could not leave this land that has belonged to us since before the white men came. It is ours, and we will not be chased off." He paused. "Besides, I wait for the day that we can take it back." He poured a warm, bitter-tasting liquid into cups for the men to drink and then continued. "They have told me I would have my own agency where my people—all my people—may live as before. Perhaps that will make a difference. General Crook has told me this."

Touch The Clouds said, "Many Indians began speaking against Crazy Horse as jealousy and distrust grew. Rumors fly concerning Crook's frequent visits to Crazy Horse's camp. They fear this relationship."

* * *

They remained in Crazy Horse's camp for the summer, and during that time, amongst rumors, lies, and deceptions, on two different occasions Four Wings rode with his friend to meet with Crook at Fort Robinson and was pleased that the meetings were cordial and both men seemed to be on good terms.

On the night of the August full moon, Four Wings and Ogden Dent set out on their way back to Canada, stopping to pay respects to Spotted Elk.

"I thank Spotted Elk for the information about the death of Eagle Feather Man. Now I must tell Gentle Breeze when we get back."

They spent a night in the camp of Spotted Elk, and the next morning they resumed their journey, arriving at Wood Mountain late the second night.

There was much rejoicing at their safe return. Four Wings and Dent were the talk of the camp, and many hours were spent with Anton, Star Woman, and Gentle Breeze as they told of what they had learned and how the people were accepting reservation life.

When it came time to tell Gentle Breeze of her father's death, Four Wings took liberties, and he told of a noble death while protecting others from a Crow war party. Four Wings saw no point in infusing her with more hatred for the army; it would do nothing but foster his own growing distaste.

* * *

September 7, 1877

About the time the sun was disappearing over the mountain, a rider rode into the camp of Eyes of Wolf. The messenger was utterly exhausted, his horse fully lathered, thoroughly spent. He was named Iron Knife, and he was from Spotted Elk's village near the Cheyenne River Agency.

"I am looking for a man named Four Wings. He travels with two women and two men. I am told he is in this encampment."

Directed to the cabin of Anton and Star Woman, the man Anton knew as Iron Knife had news. Anton gathered Four Wings and Dent together while the man ate stew left over from their late dinner.

When all were present, he began to tell the news. "Crazy Horse has been killed."

There was a general intake of air as all present gasped at the news. Four Wings was stunned. Everything and everyone around him faded to nothingness. There was no sound, nothing visible except the grain in the tabletop he sat behind. Then his hands, folded one atop the other, came into focus. Hands and woodgrain. There was a muted thumping from somewhere as his eyes were locked on those hands, and then he saw the wood hidden underneath the hands, as though they were transparent. His mind was spinning, and the sound became louder: *ka-thump, ka-thump.* Four Wings had been with Crazy Horse four weeks earlier. It made no sense. Then he heard a voice from far away: "Four Wings, Four Wings." His mind began to clear, and his surroundings became foggy, distant reality. He recognized the thumping to be his own heartbeat. He returned to the others.

He lifted his eyes and searched the faces around him.

"Four Wings, are you all right? Are you all right, my son?" Star Woman reached out to touch his arm. He responded by placing a hand on top of hers.

"Yes, Mother, I am well."

Iron Knife continued, "He went to Fort Robinson for a meeting with General Crook. He was led to a guardhouse, where he entered of his own accord. It is said that when he saw the bars on the doors and windows, he knew this was not a meeting." Iron Knife, exhausted and overcome by the story, paused while he regained control. "Those with him held him back. He fought, but they stabbed him."

Four Wings, anger mounting with every word he heard, asked, "Was Touch The Clouds with him?"

"No, Touch The Clouds rode with him but was held back when they entered."

"Do you know who entered the building with him? You said he went in without incident. You said he tried to go out." Emotion filled Four Wings when he heard the reply.

"He was with an army captain and another. Also, with his friend, Little Big Man. It is said that Little Big Man held his arms when he tried to get out the door. It was then that the army man stabbed him with his bayonet."

There was quiet in the room for a very long time. Then soft sobs could be heard from Star Woman, and Anton embraced her, pulling her close. The others stared at nothingness, their eyes seeing only a fog, their minds unable to grasp what they had just heard.

* * *

They mourned the loss of their brave friend for many days. The whole while, Four Wings wrestled with his feelings, and his heart grew heavy trying to understand the needless death he thought of as a conspiracy.

After the death of Crazy Horse, Four Wings began to spend more and more time with Sitting Bull. The passing of their friend drew them together.

Sitting Bull seemed pensive. "I feel that Crazy Horse fought against that which he could not change. If you knew Red Cloud, you would know that his victory over the Bozeman was truly a measure of his resolve to stop penetration into our hunting grounds. He had something specific to fight for—the abandonment of the Bozeman Trail." He paused, drawing a deep breath, then continued.

"That is why they called it Red Cloud's War. I feel he learned much from the Dakota war with the whites in '62. He learned from their failures. He avoided killing white women and children when he could. His war was with the army."

Four Wings listened to the man that the people revered. He directed his devotion to his people in a much different manner than did Crazy Horse, and it caused confusion in his mind. This man was not afraid to fight, yet he gave everything he owned to the people through peace, killing only when forced. Both were extraordinary men in the eyes of the people. How was this possible?

The answer came like a thunderbolt. There was one thing they had in common: both placed the good for all above their own needs. Their desire was the same—protect the people. Both believed their way to be the best way to do that. Each was true to himself.

CHAPTER TWENTY-ONE

Walker River, Nevada

1877

In Nevada, a young Indian was about to set a course that would have grave effects on the Lakota Sioux. A rancher named Dave Wilson watches his adopted son settle a wild mustang in a newly built corral. From an early age, he had shown a natural talent in calming wild horses. So impressed was Dave at that time that he encouraged the boy to hire out his gift to ranchers in the area, offering to break their horses through gentle persuasion rather than brute force.

A Paiute by birth, the lad had lost his parents, and Dave had taken him under his wing. The boy's birth name was Wovoka, but the Wilson family called him Jack.

In 1870, before he was orphaned, Wovoka had been exposed to the teachings of a Paiute medicine man named Wodziwob, and that man's teachings brought something alive within the boy. The shaman Wodziwob had a vision in which a golden age for the Indian Nations would emerge with the reappearance of the great buffalo herds of the past. For the vision to become reality, certain things needed to occur; songs, chants, and prayers were required while performing a circle dance during times of no sun—nighttime. Wodziwob's teachings were to stick in the mind of Wovoka while being reinforced through a Paiute shaman and local leader named Tävibo, who added on to Wodziwob's teachings.

The Wilsons were devout Christians, and they insisted that the young boy attend church services with them, where he acquired a belief in God and learned of Jesus Christ.

Dave Wilson stood by the corral gate as his adopted son stepped through. "Well, Jack, this is day number three for that mare. When do you figure to drop a saddle on her and see if she'll be ridden?"

"I've got no doubt that she'll let me ride her. Getting her to accept the saddle cinch and that unnatural thing on her back will be the trick. The first day I worked with her she took the bridle and allowed me to stand by her side. Tomorrow I'll be up on her without the saddle, and if that goes well, day after, she should be ready."

Regardless of the age difference, the two of them enjoyed each other's company and shared a mutual respect.

So too did the native community recognize Jack's ability to connect with animals and his growing insight into herbal cures and his ability to prophesy future events. Word was spread among the Paiute community, and through the natural course of time he began to be sought out for his knowledge by tribal members, and he was once again known as Wovoka by the tribes. He was to have his own vision, which offered a future without white dominance, and it would greatly affect the northern plains tribes.

CHAPTER TWENTY-TWO

Sitting Bull, Bill Cody, and the Ghost Dance

I n the latter part of 1879, things changed at Wood Mountain. The buffalo no longer ranged that far north because the US Army set fires to keep them south of the border.

With knowledge of the state the Indians were in, the US government offered amnesty and food to the Sioux. Emissaries for the government went into Canada and began to cause discord by telling the young Lakota that the Indians were enjoying reservation life in the United States; the government was distributing food, and the people were allowed to hunt with primitive weapons. Both appealed to the young. Discord grew.

Sitting Bull was losing favor as individuals and small groups began to wander south of the border in response to the promises made, until only a few hundred remained in Canada. The chief requested rations from the Canadian government and was turned down.

Faced with the possibility of starvation for his followers, he found himself in an untenable position. The highly respected chief made a decision.

Four Wings learned of a significant change that would greatly affect the life of the people during a late-night visit with the great chief. They were sitting at his fire when Sitting Bull spoke.

"I have made a decision. As you know, many of my young warriors have gone south to the reservation. My people will die if we stay here. I will go there also."

In 1881, with a guarantee from the government that he would not be harmed, Sitting Bull led the majority of what remained of his people back into the United States. Some elected to stay at Wood Mountain; those that returned with him were mostly the old and ill.

Upon his surrender, the government sent him and his followers to the Standing Rock Agency at Fort Yates.

The agent at the fort, James McLaughlin, wanted nothing to do with the notable chief.

"I can't have that son of a bitch at my agency. All he will do is stir up trouble. Command wants him moved to Fort Randall until the inquiry of that Custer business is complete. If we're lucky, they'll hang the bastard."

Fort Randall, on the south side of the Missouri River just north of the Nebraska border, had a much different take on the prisoner. Finding favor with the soldiers there, Sitting Bull was treated with respect, and when the government determined that he had no active part in the battle at the Little Bighorn, he was returned to Fort Yates.

McLaughlin, afraid of Sitting Bull's influence, made his life as miserable as he could while he sought his removal from the reservation. With the entire country aware of Sitting Bull's deeds, Bill Cody came calling.

"I've put together a passable performance that shows the west to the world. We get booked into places and put on a show for the people and get paid a pretty good wage for doing it. I'd like you to be part of the show."

In June 1885, Sitting Bull agreed to join Bill's traveling circus advertised as Buffalo Bill's Wild West Show. Much to McLaughlin's displeasure, virtually overnight the chief became popular with a broad swath of people, mostly white.

After few months of traveling with the show, the great chief tired of the routine and called it quits. In October, he returned to the Standing Rock

Agency, where his people welcomed him back, many coming to him for advice, again much to the chagrin of James McLaughlin.

* * *

Walker River Nevada

Wovoka's status as a medicine man had grown over the years, and his reputation had spread far beyond the Walker River region. He was wise, and men from the Paiute tribes sought his counsel.

While his mind was troubled trying to reconcile the teachings of Wodziwob and Tävibo with those of his Christian learnings, his common sense and methods of dealing with the reality of everyday life were becoming legendary. Medicine men and mystics from other tribes in areas of California, Oregon, and Nevada began to seek him out.

Like those before him, Wovoka had a vision. While Wodziwob and Tävibo envisioned the disappearance of all whites and the return of dead relatives and life lived as before the white man, Wovoka's vision was one of gaining salvation through acts of kindness and non-militaristic methods, whereby, through the round dance, they would gain a land where the buffalo would return, relatives would be resurrected, and life would be as it was before, on their own ground without white interference.

* * *

In 1889, two members of the Miniconjou Lakota traveled to Nevada to learn about the round dance and brought it back to the Pine Ridge Agency for the people to learn its magic. The version they taught was adapted to conform to the situation at hand. With the belief that the dead would be brought back, as well as other supernatural forces in play, the dance became known as the Ghost Dance.

In the Lakota version, the dancers prayed, sang songs of joy, joined hands, and began a frenetic circle dance. It was not unusual for the ill to participate in hopes of being cured, and it was not uncommon for many dancers to fall unconscious or sometimes fall into a trance as the dance progressed. As the evening wore on, the dancing stopped, and the participants sat in a circle, telling of their personal experiences during the dance and of any visions they may have had. The people on the Pine Ridge Reservation embraced the dance with absolute faith in its ability to make the prophecy a reality. They also added the element of special clothing in the form of a shirt that would protect the wearer from sickness or harm, even to the extent of stopping bullets. The people believed.

Kicking Bear, one of the Lakota who learned the dance from Wovoka, went to Standing Rock to seek Sitting Bull's permission to teach it there. Sitting Bull doubted that the dead would be brought back to life, but he had no objection to the dance itself. However, he suspected that the dance might be viewed as a threat to the Indian agencies. He was assured that if the dancers wore their Ghost Dance shirts, the soldiers' bullets would not strike them. The reaction of the white agents was one of alarm, with absolute surety that the Indians were preparing for war.

Tension increased as each new dance was performed, causing many agents to approach Washington with the request for troops to quell the dance, which they interpreted as a war dance.

* * *

It was late fall when Four Wings and Ogden Dent were talking in Four Wings's home. The two had just returned from a hunt and finished a meal made for them by Gentle Breeze.

Four Wings asked, "What are your thoughts on the value of the Ghost Dance?"

"I'm not sure you want to hear what I think. I know your people believe it will change their lives—bring back the buffalo, give them their own land, allow them to live as before the white man." There was a long pause. "Do you believe this guy in Nevada? I know Anton and your mother were involved in biblical history back in Minnesota. Do you believe this guy is the Messiah, as he claims?"

"I didn't know he made that claim. No, I don't, and I don't believe anything that anyone says the Ghost Dance will bring. I especially don't believe the ghost shirts will protect them."

Four Wings poked at the fire. "I am afraid for the people."

"I might be afraid if they didn't have common sense leaders. As long as Sitting Bull lives, his voice will bring reason. The death of Crazy Horse was terrible, but it marked the end of armed resistance by a formidable leader." Dent looked directly into the younger man's eyes. "Remember, your friend Spotted Elk, a great leader, is still there as well. He also leads the people to peace."

"I hope you're right—I hope you are right."

CHAPTER TWENTY-THREE

Standing Rock

December 15, 1890

Major James McLaughlin ordered the arrest of Sitting Bull to be carried out in the early morning. To that end, he instructed Indian reservation police to take him into custody and transport him to a specified location. Agency Police Lieutenant Bull Head led the contingent of native police. They were escorted by army troops that waited in the hills some distance away in case trouble broke out.

Sitting Bull was living in a cabin, and the reservation police approached from behind the structure without being noticed. They entered the cabin and rousted the chief from sleep. A struggle ensued when they tried to force him to go with them, as he was dressed for bed. He was allowed to throw on some clothes and was dragged out the door. During the struggle, his people were alarmed and began to gather outside the cabin, where they challenged the police to release the chief.

A shot was fired that hit Bull Head in the leg. Another of the police responded by shooting Sitting Bull in the side, and another bullet struck him in the head, killing him instantly. Firing erupted from both sides with many men dying. The soldiers charged into the action and order was restored, but many had fallen.

The bodies were loaded on a wagon and carted to Fort Yates.

At hearing of the events, McLaughlin, satisfied at what had taken place, poured a shot of whiskey and toasted to Sitting Bull's death at the hands of his own people.

* * *

Dent was south of the camp of Eyes Of Wolf to trade with the Arikara when he heard the news from a messenger from the Standing Rock Agency. The messenger was on his way to inform the Sioux who had stayed north of the border that Sitting Bull was dead.

Dent charged into the camp at Wood Mountain. Drawing his lathered horse to a stop, he swung his body to the ground and was at the door of the small cabin occupied by Four Wings and Gentle Breeze before the horse settled. Pushing through the door, he faced those inside. To his surprise, Anton and Star Woman were there visiting.

Four Wings stood up while the others stayed seated at the table in the open room. "You look like you've been riding hard. Here, have a seat." He pushed a chair in Dent's direction.

"I've got bad news." He leaned forward, hands on the chair back. "Sitting Bull has been killed at Standing Rock."

This was met by stunned silence.

Anton was the first to speak. "You say he was killed?"

Star Woman asked, "Someone killed him? It was not an accident?"

The color had left Gentle Breeze's face while her eyes were fixed firmly on Dent. Four Wings had backed against the rear wall, his mouth closed, outer edges of his lips drooping at the corners. He was numb. His mind heard the words, which kept repeating, *Sitting Bull has been killed.* There was nothing else, his mind capable only of knowing that the great chief was dead. His heart was heavy, and his chest felt empty. He slumped forward and dropped to his knees as tears flowed from his eyes. His friend, the great chief, was gone. Sorrow filled his entire being, finding release only through the tears that poured from his eyes and streamed down his face. Gentle Breeze knelt and embraced him.

Dent found his voice. "He was killed when the Indian reservation police tried to arrest him. This is bad. This is very bad."

"When did this happen?" Anton asked.

"It happened two days ago. Riders spread the news. I was in the Arikara camp when one of the messengers rode in."

"What is the reaction of the people? Surely they will not be quiet. Why were they arresting him?" Anton's mind swirled with questions. "He, like Red Cloud, would not lead warriors into battle."

Four Wings found his voice. "He knew the fight was over. Why did they kill him?" The pain in his voice was palpable. He pressed his balled fist against his thigh, rubbing absently.

"All I know is that the agent, McLaughlin, sent the Indian police to arrest him, and all hell broke loose. It had something to do with the practice of the new Ghost Dance. They wanted it stopped."

Four Wings was becoming angry. He stood. "Our leaders are dying. Our war leaders are being killed. These reservations that were set for our people are strangling them. Nothing is right." He turned to face the back wall of the cabin and thrust his open palms against the boards.

He continued as he faced the wall, "This army cannot be trusted. They have moved us to reservations where they can control us, and now they kill our leaders."

"They say the agency police killed him," Dent said. "He died at the hands of his own people."

Four Wings responded curtly, "When we were with Crazy Horse, we saw what was being done to cause friction within the people. I will not forget that." He began to pace. "There are always those that will wiggle and squirm to gain an advantage. I did not trust the Indian police then."

Anton, worried at the direction their conversation was taking, sought clarification.

"Did the messenger have any details of what happened?"

"I didn't ask questions at the time; it was such a shock." Dent tried to remember the entire conversation as it had unfolded.

"He said the police had entered Sitting Bull's cabin before sunrise and took him from his bed. When they got him outside, people began to gather, and the reservation police circled him." He paused while he searched his memory. "Someone fired a shot, followed by another, and Sitting Bull fell dead."

* * *

The Sioux at Wood Mountain mourned the passing of the great chief. They held vigils where they told and retold stories of the many sacrifices he made for his people. Late in the day, a messenger arrived with news of Sitting Bull's people at Standing Rock. He rode in well after sunset. Many had retired after dancing and celebrating Sitting Bull's life. Star Woman and Anton had retired hours ago, age bringing day's-end earlier with each passing year. Gentle Breeze had also retired to her cabin to allow the two younger men to settle a bit after the recognition and celebration of an amazing man's well-lived life.

The unknown messenger was addressing Four Wings and Ogden Dent. "The people are afraid. They are preparing to go to the camp of Spotted Elk on the Cheyenne River. The people know he is wise and will tell them what to do."

Upon hearing the news, it was as though a lightning bolt struck Four Wings.

"Of course!" Four Wings erupted. "Spotted Elk! He lives on the Cheyenne River Reservation. Why did I not think of that sooner! Sitting Bull, Crazy Horse—they're gone. Murdered. Spotted Elk is a major chief; he could be in danger right now."

"We have not heard anything about him or his people. Surely there has been no move against him," Dent said.

"Owatumla," Four Wings spoke Dent's native name. "We must go there. Surely he will listen to us and come north."

"It is doubtful that the army will allow him to leave the reservation. We must have a plan for getting him and his people to safety before more blood is shed. I think we should sleep, then figure out a way to bring them here, to Wood Mountain."

* * *

They spent the night in Dent's small cabin. Neither man slept well. Four Wings awakened to see Dent standing in front of the wood stove, a sizzling skillet on top.

"Good morning. I have meat for breakfast." Two plates appeared, and the men ate.

Dent said, "I have thought a lot since going to bed last night. The army will not like it if the people go north from the reservation land. They will surely stop them. Even if we get them here, there is not enough food to support a great number of people at Wood Mountain." He popped the last speck of meat into his mouth. "There is another alternative that makes more sense."

Four Wings listened.

"Red Cloud is much honored, and the whites leave him alone. I think Spotted Elk should go to Pine Ridge. The government will feed them, and Red Cloud will protect them."

"Will the army allow them to move?"

"I have my uniform jacket and a paper with the presidential seal giving me authority. No one knows how old it is; no one knows it dates back to President Grant." Dent looked pleased with himself. "I am confident that I can bring Spotted Elk to Pine Ridge with just a little luck on our side."

Four Wings felt a jolt of confidence and excitement. This plan was good.

* * *

December 25, 1890

Dent was speaking as the two riders emerged from the Missouri River crossing and topped the rise. It was now closing in on midnight. They had skirted the Standing Rock Agency, staying east of the Missouri. In front of them was the camp of Spotted Elk at the Cheyenne River Agency.

"This whole thing relies on passing myself off as a special agent of the president of the United States. I figure with all that's happening, I just may be able to do it." He was confident in his abilities in this regard since he had been duplicating the effort for the past several years. On occasion, they needed special consideration by the army, and Dent came through as a secret presidential emissary—never challenged—to secure that consideration.

Having participated in more than one meeting with President Grant, he was aware of army protocol and the value of being assertive. It seemed as though those with brazen disregard for common courtesy came across as senior in rank; it was particularly effective when he identified himself as a presidential emissary.

The two men were bristling with confidence as they entered the camp of Spotted Elk. Four Wings rode ahead to learn the whereabouts of their friend while Dent looked for an army authority. The confidence they held quickly vanished after hearing the news.

"We're too late. Spotted Elk left here yesterday with Sitting Bull's followers. They came to him for his counsel. They said he's heading for Pine Ridge to join Red Cloud." Four Wings was mildly encouraged.

Dent replied, "I learned that a major named Whitside is leading a regiment to locate them and bring them back to the reservation.

"There is a potential problem." Dent hesitated, clearly unwilling to say what he must. "The troops sent after them are of the 7th Cavalry. That's the same regiment whose companies the people defeated at the battle of Little Bighorn."

Four Wings, confidence dashed, was quick to answer. "I say we get a decent night's sleep, let the horses rest, and start early in the morning. We should be able to move fast with just the two of us. We need to find them before the army does."

CHAPTER TWENTY-FOUR

Wounded Knee Creek

Čhaŋkpé Ópi Wakpála

They were in the abandoned cabin of Spotted Elk. Four Wings awoke to find an empty space where Dent had spread his bedroll. Standing, he stepped to the cabin door and opened it to the pitch-black of a moonless night. A short distance away, a figure was approaching, and he soon recognized his friend. He had something in his arms.

Dent was carrying his US Army saddle, blanket, and halter. Draped over the saddle, a trooper's blue jacket was prominent. The light army saddle had been bundled and placed over the horse's withers on the ride south. It was now time to assume the role of an army officer.

"Well, you've been busy this morning."

Dent replied, "I figured if I'm the President's boy, you ought to represent an unranked army escort for someone important like me." His face broke into a broad smile.

"You figure that may keep me from getting shot?"

"It can't hurt. You are an Indian, and this just might confuse them army boys. I think you should be the invaluable scout for a pompous, incompetent white man." He pointed to the left of where they stood.

"Right there is another pile of army-issued tack. You put that on your horse, and it'll add to the confusion. These army boys are in for a visit directly from Washington."

A shrug was all he got in return as Four Wings put the items on the roan mare he had been riding for the past two decades. Before climbing aboard, he slipped into an old trooper's jacket he'd found in the cabin. Although worn and dirty, he was nonetheless thankful for the warmth it provided. By the time they were ready to go, the gray eastern sky had begun to appear beyond the horizon. As they left the camp, they did so with a feeling of uncertainty for the future; if only they had gotten there a day earlier, things would have been much better. Nudging his heels into the mare's side, Four Wings followed his friend with the realization that Owatumla looked every bit the part of a high-ranking army officer.

* * *

The two friends had been riding all day and were closing on the group ahead. Excited at the prospect of catching Spotted Elk, they stepped up the pace, wanting to overtake them before nightfall. Their excitement vanished when the trail they were following revealed the prints of many shod horses entering from the west—the 7th Cavalry was ahead of them.

Four Wings studied the tracks. "There is no sign of a battle. The way the tracks lie, the army has not caught them. See how the shod tracks eliminate those of the ponies? The only pony tracks are those on the edges where the soldiers did not ride. They have not caught up with them. It will be dark soon, and we will not be able to follow until the morning."

"We're going to find where the army is camped, and I'll talk to Major Whitside and convince him that it is in the nation's best interest to allow this band to remain with Red Cloud on this reservation and explain the folly of making them return to the Cheyenne Agency."

* * *

The inky blackness made it impossible for them to continue, so with much regret, they dismounted and, leaving the saddles in place, hobbled the horses and settled in a deep ravine they had come across. Riddled with boulders and large stones that had been moved there during the flash floods that formed the cut, the depression made the perfect shelter. At dusk, a strong wind had blown in from the northwest, and the two men huddled beneath an overhang, each wrapped in their separate bedrolls.

With the lightening of the eastern sky, they rode out of the cut and resumed following the unmistakable trail left by many riders. Within an hour, they saw a detachment of soldiers taking positions on a hillside running along a depression of sorts.

"It looks like we found the army, and it looks like they have not yet found Spotted Elk and his people." Four Wings's voice carried relief as he spoke.

The two continued to ride toward the army encampment, each searching for a shelter to indicate where the command post was set—the place they would find Major Whitside.

Dent commented, "This can't be all of them. The tracks indicated there were at least twice that many riding the trail."

Four Wings was feeling his belly begin to tighten as he sensed something was not right. "There's something strange about what we're seeing. It doesn't make sense."

The two urged their mounts into a canter, and as the distance closed, the depression beyond the hill came into view, revealing an Indian camp set alongside a meandering creek, water still running in spite of the cold.

Dent was the first to react. "Damn it, man, I'll bet that's Spotted Elk by the creek. I've got to find the major and make sure nothing happens here. I'll go to the tent yonder; why don't you ride over to the soldiers on the rise and figure out what they intend to do?"

He had just finished his instructions when a sentry popped out of nowhere.

"Halt yer progress there! Lemme see yer fingers, boys. I don't think I know you."

As they reined in and the sentry approached, it became evident that he was unsteady on his feet. "Where you be from?"

"We rode in from east of here looking for whoever is in command." Dent was entering his role. Dismounting, he stepped to the sentry and, from a distance of about three inches, whispered into his face. "You better have a damn good reason for stopping me, mister. I am here under the authority of the president of the United States." He paused and sniffed the air. "You been drinking, man?"

"Just a little, sir. We got us a renegade Injun down to the creek there. Figure it's one o' them what kilt Custer."

"Don't you know it's against regs to drink on duty, soldier?"

"Yes, sir, we's jest celebratin' catchin' these damn Injuns. They's the same 'uns what kilt Custer a while back. Colonel Forsyth hisself took a drink or two. We come to disarm this camp and take all of 'em in and lock 'em up."

"Is Forsyth in command here?"

"Damn straight, and he's one hell of an officer—sir!"

"Is that his command tent?" Dent pointed.

"Yes, sir."

"Hand me your rifle, soldier." Reaching out, he grabbed it from the man's hands and, without a word, spun it and rammed the butt end into the center of the man's face, dropping him on the spot.

"I hope I killed him. These boys are liquored up—hard telling what could happen. I'm going to find this Forsyth and put an end to this before things go bad. You might just ride up behind them on the hill over there and stand ready."

With rifle in hand, he mounted his horse and rode toward the man he believed to be Colonel Forsyth.

Four Wings felt a chill starting in the pit of his stomach that radiated up his torso as the hair on the back of his neck stood on end, and it was as though his scalp was immersed in ice water. He stood, rooted in place, unable to make his legs carry him to his horse.

He turned to watch Owatumla ride away, and whatever spell had overtaken him was broken. Grabbing the saddle horn, he swung himself up and reined her to approach the hill from the back. Once on the crest, he stopped to see what would transpire.

On the other side of a cleared area toward the south of where they had ridden in, he saw Dent dismount and approach a man in the center of several other troopers.

Refocusing his attention to the creek bottom and the small camp resting there, he saw several troopers standing around a growing mound of something as other troopers added to a pile near the center of the camp. More soldiers appeared to go into a tipi, staying inside for only a few moments, and then reappearing to move to the next one.

Moments passed before he realized they were collecting the firearms from the camp. He knew that the next step was to take the horses, leaving the camp without mounts. It was the same thing that had been done to every band that entered the reservation.

Looking back at Dent, he saw the two men seemed to be in an animated argument as fingers pointed and tensions appeared to rise. Once again looking to the center of the camp, he saw a trooper approaching one of the Indians who was holding a rifle. Reaching for it, the trooper and the Indian began to struggle, and a shot rang out.

Four Wings's eyes snapped back to where Dent had been arguing, but he was no longer there, and the men had all drawn their pistols. He saw something lying on the ground, but before he could focus, the world exploded.

He stared, unbelieving, at what was taking place below. Brave men, men with peaceful intent, were being slaughtered indiscriminately. Women and children were raked with shrapnel as the Hotchkiss guns opened fire on the weaponless braves now running for their lives. Small bodies were trampled under hooves lined with steel, and blood covered the ground.

Then there was silence, absolute silence, as though his ears were stuffed with clay. He surveyed the scene where the carnage continued. He saw the smoke from the big guns and that from the firearms carried by the troopers, but there was no sound. The open mouths of innocent women screaming for their children were silent. He leaned over and retched as sweat froze on his forehead.

He reined his horse, nudged her side with his heels, and began to move to the north, the cacophony of slaughter again ringing in his ears, totally unable to process what was happening. For the first forty yards or so, he walked the roan mare. Within one hundred yards, she was at a dead run as tears cut paths through the icy skin on his temples. He had seen death a hundred ways, had taken many lives himself, but this was something his mind could not grasp. This was not battle; there was no honor in killing the innocent. Every fiber of his existence screamed for release from the scene that left him in agony.

The mare stumbled, nearly unseating her rider, and he pulled on the reins, slowing her to a canter, then to a walk. Her withers and neck were lathered as steam created an aura surrounding the two. He dismounted and unstrapped the army saddle, throwing it to the ground, followed by the blue trooper's jacket he was wearing, exposing the buckskin shirt he wore beneath. He then wiped her dry with the blanket and removed the bridle, replacing it with a solitary piece of rawhide looped around her muzzle and knotted to her mane. He grabbed his bedroll from the saddle, and they walked, man and horse; she, cooling down; he, trying to purge his mind of what he had witnessed.

He walked without thought as the sky began to boil. He paid no mind. After considerable time had gone by and he had continued to walk absently, the sky unleashed a terrible wind, and snow pelted his face. He didn't notice.

It was the next morning before his mind returned to the here-and-now. It was as though he had just awakened from a dream. Nothing registered; nothing made sense. *How did I get here? Where am I?* His mind wasn't working.

Looking around, he realized he was in a shallow wash; the mare stood a few feet away, halter strap trailing on the ground as she calmly watched him. Somehow he had wrapped his bedroll around himself and crawled into a depression left when a boulder had been washed from the sidewall of the ravine. He was on the leeward side of the cut. The opposite side was snow covered; while his position was cold, at least it was dry.

His mind brought him back to the atrocity he had witnessed, and he found it impossible to move. So he lay there, haunted by what he had seen, his mind hearing the explosions and screams while the image of his friend, Ogden Dent—Owatumla, lay on the ground surrounded by blue-coated devils.

Finally, after a very long time, he moved from his safe spot and led the roan out of the gully. Reliant on dead reckoning, he swung onto her back and headed north, filled with fear of the future and harboring a newfound hatred for the army.

CHAPTER TWENTY-FIVE

The Aftermath

S pring was in the air as Four Wings poked at the coals inside the small woodstove that warmed their cabin. He picked up a piece of wood split from a larger section and added it to the glowing embers. Since his return, his mind had fixated on a growing hatred for the white man. All the bad that had been dealt his people started with the US Army and their overbearing need to control and conquer, taking everything of value and leaving table scraps for his people. There was no compromise in their methods, and he would offer no compromise in his growing hate.

As January turned to February, his outlook began to affect his relationship with Gentle Breeze. The transition from February to March found them arguing about things that should have no consequnce to their relationship. Four Wings talked of nothing but his building rage and deepening hate. Try as she did to turn the subject to their daily needs and discussions meaningful to their life together, he unfailingly turned to the fire he held within. It became so bad that he stopped talking to her. Anton offered nothing but excuses for wrongs done. Only his mother, Star Woman, seemed to understand his hatred aimed at the whites.

It was as though there was nothing else he could think about. The family began to distance themselves from him. Gentle Breeze eventually moved to the cabin of Star Woman and Anton forty feet away, and he was alone with his thoughts.

On a summer day, when the women were at a function in the town of Wood Mountain, Four Wings knocked on Anton's door.

"May I come in?"

"Certainly, would you like to share some tea with me?" Anton, surprised yet pleased that Four Wings came to visit, approached hoping to embrace the son he had taken as his own those many years ago. Four Wings stood stiffly, offering his hand.

"That would be fine."

Anton took the offered hand.

Four Wings surveyed the interior as though it was his first time in the small cabin. "Where does Gentle Breeze sleep?"

Anton's mind recoiled from the sharp tone of his adopted son's voice. "We have a blanket that separates her sleeping area from the rest." *That was a strange question.* "Would you like a little sugar in your tea? It sweetens it up." He charged forward to keep the conversation pointed in the right direction. "I'm glad to see you here. It is wonderful to talk to you; it's been a while, so I know you must be a busy man. Gentle Breeze mentioned that you might be interested in working in the fields for one of the local farmers."

"That's what she said?"

"Well, not in so many words, but that's what I heard. She said that the locals are looking for help with their harvest."

"Well, you heard wrong. I'd rather starve than work for a white man."

"Do you think that might be a bit extreme?"

"I suppose you don't think it was a bit extreme when they stole our land! Was it a bit extreme when they killed Crazy Horse? When they murdered Sitting Bull?" Anton was taken aback. With each question, the voice became louder.

"It certainly wasn't a bit extreme when they stole Pahá Sápa after agreeing it was ours forever into the future?"

"Simmer down, son. Of course those were all bad things. No one will deny that."

"Don't call me son! I am not your son, and I'm tired of hearing you make excuses for what the white man has done." Four Wings's face was turning red, and a prominent neck vein was becoming enlargd. "I can't even say 'white' without hate bubbling to the surface. I hate them for what they have done, and I will always hate them."

Anton approached and placed his hand on the younger man's shoulder. "Son, your hate is controlling—"

"Get your hand off me! Don't you ever touch me!" He slapped the hand away with such force that Anton lost his balance and fell against the table. "I came here so we could start fresh. It was a mistake."

"Four Wings, I think you should leave. I think you should go away—someplace, anyplace where you can think clearly. Your hate is eating you up, destroying your marriage."

"Don't you worry about me, old man." He pulled the door open and stepped outside. "You won't see me again."

He stormed to his cabin and began to bundle things for a journey. A half hour later, he left the cabin, cut the hobble on his horse, and rode away, bristling with anger.

* * *

Anton and the two women talked often about Four Wings, not knowing exactly where he was. Star Woman often heard Gentle Breeze cry herself to sleep. The young woman was anguished at the change in her husband and prayed to the Great Spirit that he would find forgiveness in his heart and become what he had been.

It was Star Woman's opinion that her son would come to his senses if left alone. He was a good man, and she spent many days remembering the past and his attachment to her husband. They had been so close.

Anton's health began a downward spiral the winter that Four Wings left. His leg began to ache, and he found it difficult to walk. There was an early thaw in 1893, and they learned from trappers that Four Wings was in the hills less than a day's ride west. The men were from a settlement several days' ride west of Wood Mountain. They sold furs at Wood Mountain, and when they left to return to their homes, Star Woman asked them to tell Four Wings that Anton was very sick.

Anton died in March of 1893, four months before his eighty-eighth birthday. He had a Christian burial at Star Woman's insistence. She got no answer from Four Wings, and he was not present at the funeral, which weighed heavily on her.

After a month passed, she approached Gentle Breeze with a request that she ride with her to find her son. The younger woman was quick to agree. The two of them left for the mountain where they heard he was living. It was a scant eighteen miles away.

The reunion was clumsy, and when Four Wings learned that Anton had died, he became angry. Holding on to his anger from the deaths of his friends, he was ill-equipped to handle the news of another death. There were no tears; only rage bubbled to the surface. He was shaken to the core. Unable to face his mother, he looked upon Gentle Breeze, and with profound sadness disguised as anger, he left the cabin and didn't return. The two women waited for hours, and still he didn't return. Finally, as the new day broke, they left the cabin and returned to the Wood Mountain settlement.

Four Wings didn't return to his cabin until four days had passed. His mind was awash with conflicting emotions, and he focused on the death of each of his friends one at a time, trying to make sense of each. At the center of all, he recognized the greed of the white man. Every one of them was evil and couldn't be trusted.

Eagle Feather Man. The army killed his eagle, and then they killed him when he objected.

Crazy Horse. A great warrior chief. Not given a chance to die a warrior's death. Killed at the hands of the army because they feared him. Four Wings's mind boiled with raw hate.

Sitting Bull was a wise chief, big medicine, brother to all. Even the white man. Why did he die? Because he was strong, they feared his influence with the people. They killed him like they killed Crazy Horse, when he was alone.

These things repeated over and over in his mind. He was tired, he was angry, and he couldn't clear them out of his thoughts.

Then something happened.

He remembered Ogden Dent—Owatumla. He was a white man, yet he died the death of an Indian. He died at the hands of the army while trying to save the life of an Indian. *How to reconcile this?* He then thought of the great chief that had won his fight against the white army, Red Cloud. Here was a man that now lived in peace after winning his war. What was the reason for this? How could this have come to be?

His mind was scrambled, his nerves raw, yet he refused to look beyond his pain for answers. He remembered when they first met Spotted Elk upon arriving at the Black Hills. Now he too was dead. Murdered—no, slaughtered by the US Army while under a flag of truce. Wave after wave of nausea overcame him as his stomach cramped and his heart ached with the hate he felt.

The weeks passed; February turned to March, March to April. The whole time, Four Wings stayed in the cabin, leaving only to relieve himself or retrieve an animal from one of three snares he set in view of the cabin window.

He searched deep into his soul for answers to questions he was afraid to ask. He found himself remembering those he had killed in battle during the Minnesota uprising and his near brush with death during the same period. He remembered when he was a child, Anton and his friend had taken him on a hunt for white-tailed deer, and he had failed miserably. But Anton was patient, and the child had learned.

He remembered the friend on the hunt was a white man, a good white man. He began to search his past for white people that were good people, those that showed no bias because of skin color. Less and less often did his mind bring him to the deaths of his friends. Deaths he did not witness, deaths that were told of by others.

More and more often the vision of his white friend, Owatumla, lying at the feet of a colonel named Forsyth came to the fore. He had given his life trying to save Spotted Elk.

He remembered what Anton had said to him before he rode with Crazy Horse to Sitting Bull's camp on the Rosebud. When no one else wanted him to go, Anton had given his permission. The words were etched permanently into his memory. *"Go. Then decide if your life will make a difference. I say your death will do nothing to preserve our way of life, but your living means there is a chance for all of us."*

Then his mind turned to his mother. Star Woman. She was possibly the strongest woman he had ever known. Somehow, she saw good in the heart of the enemy.

Slowly, guilt began to replace the hate he felt. Guilt replaced his anger and filled him with sadness beyond what he had ever before experienced. He remembered his last words spoken to the man he respected more than anyone in the world. *"You won't see me again."* He clenched his jaw as a tear ran down his cheek.

The following weeks passed, and the mind of Four Wings vacillated wildly yet steadily in the direction that seemed to offer it peace. His memories of good things began to displace the hate he had harbored. He felt a physical healing coming over him.

On the morning that the change occurred, it was like a sudden starburst. Four Wings's entire mindset seemed to flip, and what he saw before him was a future with hope, and he realized something.

He realized his heart, filled with hate as it was, was incapable of allowing any other emotion. It was holding him captive. The hatred he had harbored had taken control of his life; he had attacked those he loved.

For the first time in a long time, he remembered the beautiful Gentle Breeze and their time alone. He thought of the many white men he had met that were honorable and human, with human faults like everyone in the world. He realized that past wrongs could never be taken away; there was no going back, only forward.

With this understanding, everything changed. A burden was lifted, replaced by hope. The anger and hurt that had taken over were gone. Gone was his guilt.

His heart opened to possibilities for the future. A future filled with promise. He remembered what Anton had told him a long time ago, *"You must follow your heart; it will guide you."* By putting the past behind him. By accepting and forgiving past wrongs, for the first time in a long, long time, he missed Gentle Breeze as he contemplated their future together.

* * *

He rode through the night, unsure of what the new day would bring. Dawn was nudging the horizon in front of him. He had reined his roan mare to a standstill as he looked toward the buildings he had called home, the buildings he, Anton, and Owatumla had built together.

He urged the mare forward and once again walked toward the buildings when a door opened and someone appeared. She walked confidently forward, then stopped when she saw him. He sat, unsure at what she may do.

Gentle Breeze looked toward the single rider. It seemed that a lifetime passed between them before he saw her drop the pail she was carrying. He swung down off the mare's back, and he heard a barely perceptible squeal as she ran barefoot toward him. They met in a passionate embrace as the melody of a cardinal warbled from the trees, greeting the new day.

THE END

Study References

It is essential in uncovering the truth to take the initiative and pull multiple references from different sources since many offer contradictory evidence spoken as fact. As in all things human, we must search for the explanation evidenced by common sense and multiple source reassurance.

References:

The Fort Laramie Treaties of 1851 & 1868
https://www.ndstudies.gov/gr8/content/unit-iii-waves-development-1861-1920/lesson-4-alliances-and-conflicts/topic-2-sitting-bulls-people/section-3-treaties-fort-laramie-1851-1868

Concerning The Bozeman Trail & Fetterman Fight
https://www.wyohistory.org/encyclopedia/brief-history-bozeman-trail

http://www.wyomingtalesandtrails.com/ftkearney.html

https://www.wyohistory.org/sites/default/files/crook2.jpg

https://en.wikipedia.org/wiki/Fort_Reno_(Wyoming)#/media/File:Bozeman01.png

http://www.historynet.com/red-cloud

http://www.pbs.org/weta/thewest/people/i_r/redcloud.htm

https://www.britannica.com/biography/Red-Cloud-Sioux-chief

http://www.history.com/this-day-in-history/indians-massacre-fetterman-and-eighty-soldiers

http://www.friendslittlebighorn.com/Fetterman-Battle.htm

http://native-american-indian-facts.com/Famous-Native-American-Facts/Chief-Red-Cloud-Facts.shtml

Illegal War and Grant's Cabal To Claim The Black Hills
https://www.smithsonianmag.com/history/ulysses-grant-launched-illegal-war-plains-indians-180960787/

* Read the historical reenactment.

The Death Of Crazy Horse
http://www.history.com/topics/native-american-history/crazy-horse

http://www.american-tribes.com/Lakota/BIO/CrazyHorse-Part1.htm

http://www.historynet.com/crazy-horse

* Read the historical reenactment.

Timeline – War with the Sioux Nation

1862 AUGUST–DECEMBER – Dakota (Sioux) Uprising, Minnesota.

1866 JULY – Red Cloud's War on Bozeman Trail, Montana Territory, begins.

DECEMBER 21 – Fetterman Fight, Montana Territory.

1868 NOVEMBER 4 – Chief Red Cloud signs Fort Laramie Treaty, ending Red Cloud's War.

1869 SUMMER – Sitting Bull elected head chief of non-reservation Lakota.

1874 JULY –AUGUST – Custer discovers gold in the Black Hills.

1875 NOVEMBER 3 – President Grant convenes secret White House meeting to plan strategy for provoking war with the Lakota.

1876 MARCH 17 – Battle of Powder River, Montana Territory.

EARLY JUNE – Lakota and Northern Cheyenne hold joint Sun Dance at Deer Medicine Rocks, Montana Territory.

JUNE 17 – Battle of the Rosebud, Montana Territory.

JUNE 25 – Battle of the Little Bighorn, Montana Territory.

SEPTEMBER – Reservation Lakota chiefs relinquish the Unceded Indian Territory.

1877 MAY 6 – Crazy Horse surrenders at Fort Robinson, Nebraska.

MAY 7 – Sitting Bull enters Canada.

1881 JULY 20 – Sitting Bull surrenders at Fort Buford, Dakota Territory.

1883 MAY 10 – Sitting Bull becomes an "agency Indian" on the Great Sioux Reservation.

1889 JUNE – Sioux Land Commission breaks up the Great Sioux Reservation.

1890 DECEMBER 15 – Sitting Bull is killed on the Standing Rock Reservation, North Dakota.

DECEMBER 29 – Tragedy at Wounded Knee Creek, Pine Ridge Reservation, South Dakota.

1891 JANUARY 15 – Brulé and Oglala Lakota surrender at Pine Ridge Agency, South Dakota.

The following are historical reenactments I believe reflect the facts surrounding these incidents, supported by multiple study references.

* Illegal War and Grant's Cabal To Claim The Black Hills

President Ulysses S. Grant sat across the table from Commanding General of the Army William Tecumseh Sherman. Since the two men had been united during the War Between the States, their political views regarding the Indian had resulted in a schism between them.

Grant was speaking, "Of course we want to keep the peace, but we cannot allow the Indians to stop our progress as a nation."

Sherman countered, "It's my opinion that the leaders of the tribes seek only to be left to their own devices without the government dictating their future to them."

"You know me, when it comes to war, I am a hawk. When it comes to peace, I offer my hand." Grant was proud of the reputation he had gained as an aggressive leader; he was also viewed as one who wanted peace with the Indians, having taken office in 1869 on a promise to keep the West free of war. He was on record as saying, "Our dealings with the Indians properly lay us open to charges of cruelty and swindling," an explicit reference to prior administrations and his current rival for the presidency.

Sherman replied, "As it should be. Our treaty signed at Fort Laramie two years ago states the position of the government clearly when it says all war between the parties to this agreement shall forever cease. To our credit, I believe we have been, for the most part, faithful to that."

"And so it shall remain."

Sherman continued, "We cannot ignore the fact that this treaty, signed one year before you took office, promised the Lakota absolute and undisturbed occupation of the land we call the Great Sioux Reservation."

President Grant, unperturbed, nodded his acquiescence.

The men continued to discuss the situation with the expansion of the rail lines westward as well as matters of national interest regarding what was turning into a potential crisis surrounding funding for the government and the burgeoning economic depression.

* * *

To the north, at Fort Abraham Lincoln, Lieutenant Colonel George A. Custer was second in command under Colonel David Stanley as they prepared to move west to "ensure the safety" of surveyors for the Northern Pacific Railroad. Referred to as the Yellowstone Expedition, the accompanying military escort consisted of over fifteen hundred soldiers. The resistance they encountered, and it was significant, was offered by Sitting Bull, Gall, Crazy Horse, and warriors from Hunkpapa, Oglala, Miniconjou, and Cheyenne tribes.

The military escort was deemed necessary because of attacks made a year earlier when a similar survey party encountered Sitting Bull and Crazy Horse leading opposition to the survey crew. During that encounter, Major E. M. Baker, in command of nearly four hundred troops, fought to a standstill with forces under the leadership of Sitting Bull and Crazy Horse. Although there was no clear victor in that battle, it buoyed the confidence of the Indians to hold off a westward movement of the white invaders to their ancestral lands.

There were other skirmishes between the US Army and the Indian Nations over the next few years, primarily caused by bad blood on both sides.

The combination of the closing of the Bozeman Trail and the goldfields playing out resulted in a decrease of conflicts between Indians and whites. The signing of a new Fort Laramie treaty in 1868 stopped the raids on wagon trains moving west.

The majority of Lakota bands chose to live on the reservation and accept the government dole that came with it. During the next few years, several bands preferred living in the unceded land west of the Great Sioux Reservation. Joining Red Cloud, Sitting Bull, and Crazy Horse were additional Lakota as well as bands from the Northern Cheyenne and Arapaho Nations. They moved among the vast buffalo herds, living as they had always lived.

The presence of the transcontinental railroad south of the Platte River began to thin the buffalo herds when soldiers and settlers began killing them by the thousands. The correspondence between William Tecumseh Sherman and Philip Sheridan in 1868 before the signing of the Fort Laramie Treaty was taking place reveals much.

In a private correspondence dated May 10, 1868, Commanding General of the US Army William Tecumseh Sherman wrote to General Phillip Sheridan, Commander of the Department of the Missouri, that as long as buffalo roamed parts of Nebraska, "Indians will go there. I think it would be wise to invite all the sportsmen of England and America there this fall for a Grand Buffalo hunt and make one grand sweep of them all."

In October 1868, Sheridan wrote to Sherman that their best hope to control the Native Americans was to "make them poor by the destruction of their stock, and then settle them on the lands allotted to them."

Red Cloud signed the Fort Laramie Treaty of 1868 on November 4 of that year. It contained a clause designating the land north of the North Platte River from the western limit of the new reservation, farther west to the Bighorn Mountains as Unceded Indian Territory. Although undefined, the northern boundary came to be considered as the Yellowstone River.

Ceded land meant that it was turned over to another. The vagueness of the term "Unceded Indian Territory" left much room for interpretation. Adding to the confusion was a clause found in the provision that no whites would be permitted to settle in the Unceded Indian Territory without Indian permission. Lakota lands were to be inviolate, the peace permanent. Red Cloud had won his war. Whether he would prevail in peace, only time would tell.

What was left open for interpretation were unclear rights and restrictions pertaining to the Indians who wished to refuse government subsidies and live off the hunt in Unceded Territory and their legal right to reside there.

The Sioux who had preferred to stay off the government reservations by making their homes in the unceded territory were the first to be alarmed at what was taking place in clear violation of the treaty, as they saw it. Ulysses S. Grant was about to embark on a secret agenda intending to take the Black Hills from the Sioux by force.

His campaign promise to keep the West free of war meant that any hostilities that might develop must be started by the Sioux; any ensuing military operation by the United States would then be viewed as a justifiable retaliatory action.

* * *

Philip Sheridan was appointed to command the Military Division of the Missouri shortly after Grant's ascension to the presidency. In that capacity, all the Great Plains fell under his command. By October 1875, Grant had ordered Lt. General Sheridan to come to Washington. For reasons known only to Grant, the order bypassed Sheridan's immediate superior, William Tecumseh Sherman. Grant was about to put his plan for taking the Black Hills in motion.

The elite group of men chosen for the task had one thing in common. While some were competent military planners in Grant's estimation, each of them viewed the Indian problem as one that could be solved with force.

On November 3, they assembled in a small office in Washington; Sherman was unaware, having moved his headquarters from Washington to St. Louis after a strong disagreement with Grant. In a direct disregard of protocol, the cabal included two men under Sherman's command, Lieutenant General Philip Sheridan and Brigadier General George Crook. Also included in the group was the Secretary of War, William Belknap; Grant's newly appointed Secretary of the Interior, Zachariah Chandler, a former senator from Michigan and hardliner on Indian affairs; and the assistant Interior Secretary, Benjamin R. Cowen. The final member of the cabal was the Commissioner of Indian Affairs, Edward P. Smith.

"Men, this can't be made public, so we must keep it under our hats." Grant began the meeting. "We've got one hell of a problem with the financial downturn that's settled over the nation since the war. Now we find a bonanza of gold in the Black Hills, and we can't touch it without starting a war with the Sioux."

All members present were aware of the situation.

"We could move in and take it, but the general public will never settle for that." There were nods all around. "What we need to do is get a war started without it appearing we caused the damn thing."

They were developing a plan to take the Black Hills while feeding a public script to the press and Congress.

The conspirators believed that the non-treaty Lakotas—those living in Unceded Territory—under the leadership of Sitting Bull, had intimidated the reservation chiefs and convinced them to avoid signing any agreement with the whites that would in any way allow them into Pahá Sápa. The consensus of the conspirators was that if the non-treaty bands were beaten, the reservation chiefs would yield and relinquish mining rights.

The solution was obvious; eliminate the Indians living on unceded land. To this end, the plan was to issue an edict that could not, or would not be complied with, namely, demand that all Indians return to their respective reservation land or be considered hostile and face the might of the US Army. It was believed that Sitting Bull, Crazy Horse, and the other chiefs living in the unceded territory would reject this ultimatum.

On December 3, Sitting Bull and the other chiefs that had not signed the treaty and lived on unceded land were told that they had until January 31 to report to the reservation. An impossible task since most were widely scattered and snowbound.

Due to the weather conditions, the government attempts to enforce the edict were ineffective, but the die had been cast, and the stage was set.

* Death of Crazy Horse

On May 6, 1877, Crazy Horse surrendered himself and his band at Fort Robinson, where the army took their guns and horses, as they had done to all non-reservation Indians. The band was allowed to set their camp while remaining under control of the military. As the weeks passed and the Indians realized that the army was in control and their lot could be improved by gaining favor with those in power, individual segments of the captives stirred trouble while trying to ingratiate themselves to the whites. Gossip, backbiting, deceit, and betrayal began to spread among the people.

General Crook met with Crazy Horse on multiple occasions to talk about a promised Crazy Horse Agency location and details surrounding reservation life. In July, the Nez Perce Indians left their reservation and headed northeast through Montana with the intent of fleeing into Canada. In defiance of all logic, Crook wanted Crazy Horse to lead his warriors to control the Nez Perce. His ongoing attempts to convince him were always met with a refusal.

Crazy Horse's answer was always the same. "When I came to you, I promised to make no more war."

General Crook instructed a young Lieutenant Clark to continue to press for the Oglala Lakota chief's help.

Many Indians began speaking against Crazy Horse as jealousy and distrust continued to mount. An Indian named Woman Dress came to Crook with the false story that Crazy Horse planned to kill him during an upcoming meeting. Crook chose to communicate with the Indian through a third party.

A scout named Frank Grouard was chosen by Crook to act as liaison during these meetings and report the proceedings. Grouard was not a Native, but through circumstance had lived in the camps of Crazy Horse and Sitting Bull in years past and, unknown to Crazy Horse, had been present at the Battle of the Rosebud, where he was General Crook's chief scout.

For Crazy Horse, the frustration grew with the ongoing requests for his involvement in settling the Nez Perce situation until he finally lost patience and, in reply to Grouard's plea, finally gave the answer they sought.

"You do not hear me when I tell you I will not fight. Now I tell you I will fight the Nez Perce, but if I go to fight, I will fight until the Nez Perce are all dead and they are no more. Is that what is wanted?"

Grouard was afraid of what Crazy Horse would do to him if he learned of his tenure with Crook as a scout at the Rosebud. He thought his life could be extended if Crazy Horse was removed from the equation, so, in his report to General Crook, Grouard changed the words that he had delivered. "Crazy Horse said he would fight until every last white man was killed." Crook, upon hearing that, decided that the Indian chief was too dangerous to be allowed to walk freely and must be placed behind locked doors.

The next day, Crazy Horse was led into a building thinking he was going to meet General Bradley. Before entering, he looked into the distance to see Touch the Clouds coming toward him. Upon entering the door, he saw bars on the windows, and he knew things were not right.

Turning, he lunged toward the door, but Little Big Man grabbed him by both arms and held him back. Struggling to get free, Crazy Horse was able to draw his knife and slash Little Big Man's hand. It was then that Private William Gentles stabbed Crazy Horse with his bayonet, and the great chief slumped to the ground.

Touch the Clouds had reached the building in time to see Crazy Horse, his cousin, friend, and chief, fall to his knees. Orders were given to move him into the guardhouse, but Touch the Clouds pleaded that Crazy Horse was a great chief and could not be placed in prison.

Now, surrounded by reservation Indians, better judgment came to the fore, and Touch The Clouds was allowed to carry him into the adjutant's office and lay him on the floor while the camp doctor, trusted by Crazy Horse, administered a shot of morphine to ease the pain. A short while later Crazy Horse's father, Worm, arrived to be with his son.

At about 11:30 that night, September 5, 1877, Crazy Horse died.

General Refrences

Several references steer you to additional information. For a better understanding of events, it is hoped you will delve beyond what I have listed here.

https://www.legendsofamerica.com/na-siouxwars/

http://www.eyewitnesstohistory.com/knee.htm

http://www.stmuhistorymedia.org/the-ghost-dance-and-wounded-knee-massacre/

https://www.ndstudies.gov/gr8/content/unit-iii-waves-development-1861-1920/lesson-4-alliances-and-conflicts/topic-2-sitting-bulls-people/section-5-battle-rosebud-and-little-big-horn

http://www.woodmountain.ca/history/index.html

Wovoka
http://www.u-s-history.com/pages/h3770.html

Our Indian Wards – George Manypenny
https://ia600202.us.archive.org/21/items/cu31924088025014/cu31924088025014.pdf

Indian Heros and Great Chieftains
https://archive.org/details/indianheroes00eastrich

Bury My Heart At Wounded Knee – Dee Brown, pub. Henry Holt & Co. Sitting Bull
http://www.u-s-history.com/pages/h3771.html

Native American History – Sitting Bull
https://www.history.com/topics/native-american-history/sitting-bull

Biography of Sitting Bull
https://www.biography.com/people/sitting-bull-9485326

Chief Sitting Bull – Lakota Nation – Daniel N. Paul
http://www.danielnpaul.com/ChiefSittingBull-LakotaNation.html

Sitting Bull Leads his People Into Canada
http://www.history.com/this-day-in-history/sitting-bull-leads-his-people-into-canada

The history and culture of the Standing Rock Oyate
http://www.ndstudies.org/resources/IndianStudies/standingrock/historical_intro.html

Sibley and Sully Expeditions
http://history.nd.gov/historicsites/sibleysully/history1.html

General Alfred Sully's Expedition of 1864
http://genealogytrails.com/ndak/dunn/military/military_1864expedition.html

Smithsonian—How The Battle Of The Little Bighorn Was Won
file:///Users/daleswanson/Desktop/Novel%20Sequel/***Indian-Battle%20of%20Little%20Bighorn%20Smithsonian.webarchive

A Brief History of the Bozeman Trail
https://www.wyohistory.org/encyclopedia/brief-history-bozeman-trail

Sand Creek Massacre
https://www.smithsonianmag.com/history/horrific-sand-creek-massacre-will-be-forgotten-no-more-180953403/

Lower Yellowstone Project

https://www.usbr.gov/gp/mtao/loweryellowstone/ea_amended/app_h.pdf

I have many more references that I used as research. To check them all would require you to spend many, many hours looking into each because each will lead to more.